***"I don't know wh***

***here..."***

he whispered thickly against her throat, "but I know where it's going if you don't say stop damned quick."

"I don't want to stop. I want you."

Sophie knew she hadn't said that. Another woman in the room had. A stranger, a completely immoral, amoral stranger.

The same stranger pushed at his sweater, took his mouth as avidly, as hungrily, as he took hers. Beneath the wool was hair-roughened skin, the ripple of muscle and sinew, nothing soft. She demanded bare flesh, needing to touch him. Everywhere. Anywhere. When he started raining kisses down her throat, she nipped at his shoulder. Just little bites.

He tasted damned good.

"Where did all this come from?" he muttered. "I thought you were shy."

Dear Reader,

Years ago I wrote four romantic-suspense novels and always wanted to write more…just never had a chance. *Secretive Stranger* is the first in a Silhouette Romantic Suspense trilogy.

This one is Sophie's story. As she and her sisters know well, sometimes you just can't recover if your whole life was uprooted at a very young age. Sophie doesn't willingly trust anyone or anything.

Cord starts out less a hero than a cattle prod. He isn't who he says he is, and he can't—or isn't—telling her the truth. He's the last man Sophie could possibly trust….but the one man she must trust, to heal her heart and reach out for love.

I hope you love the story—I loved writing it!

Jennifer Greene

# JENNIFER GREENE

*Secretive Stranger*

ROMANTIC
SUSPENSE

Recycling programs for this product may not exist in your area.

ISBN-13: 978-0-373-27675-2

SECRETIVE STRANGER



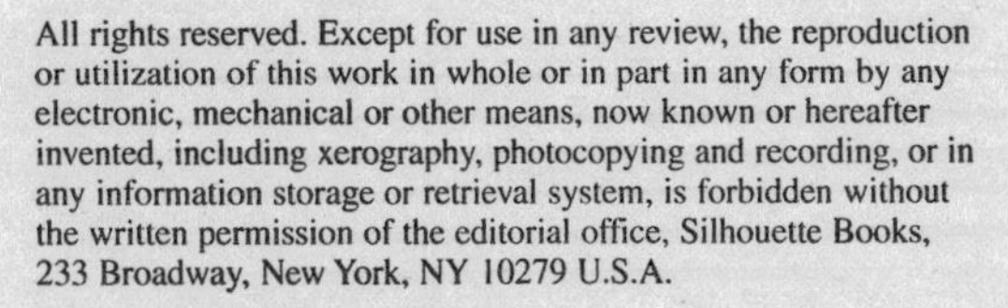


This edition published by arrangement with Harlequin Books S.A.

For questions and comments about the quality of this book please contact us at Customer_eCare@Harlequin.ca.



Visit Silhouette Books at www.eHarlequin.com

**Printed in U.S.A.**

**Books by Jennifer Greene**

Silhouette
Romantic Suspense

*Secrets* #221
*Devil's Night* #305
*Broken Blossom* #345
*Pink Topaz* #418
‡‡*Secretive Stranger* #1605

Silhouette Special Edition

**The 200% Wife* #1111

Silhouette Books

*Birds, Bees and Babies*
"Riley's Baby"

*Santa's Little Helpers*
"Twelfth Night"

*The Stanford Sisters
**Body & Soul
††Happily Ever After
‡The Scent of Lavender
‡‡New Man in Town

Silhouette Desire

††*Prince Charming's Child* #1225
††*Kiss Your Prince Charming* #1245
***Rock Solid* #1316
*Millionaire M.D.* #1340
‡*Wild in the Field* #1545
‡*Wild in the Moonlight* #1588
‡*Wild in the Moment* #1622
*Hot to the Touch* #1670
*The Soon-To-Be-Disinherited Wife* #1731

---

## *JENNIFER GREENE*

lives near Lake Michigan with her husband and an assorted menagerie of pets. Michigan State University has honored her as an outstanding woman graduate for her work with women on campus.

Jennifer has written more than seventy love stories, for which she has won numerous awards, including four RITA® Awards from the Romance Writers of America and both their Hall of Fame and Lifetime Achievement Awards.

You're welcome to contact Jennifer through her Web site at www.jennifergreene.com.

To the infamous Creative Festers, whose love and support are unique in the universe.
You're beyond wonderful!

## *Chapter 1*

One more block. That's all Sophie Campbell had to walk. All right, so maybe it was pouring rain and she was juggling a satchel of heavy books and an overfilled grocery bag. So maybe she never dreamed October nights could be this cold in Virginia, and she was soaked to the bone, and darn it, her feet hurt. Still…she could make it that last block, couldn't she?

A fat, pretty orange bounced out of the grocery sack and rolled down the sidewalk. When she instinctively shifted to grab it, a head of lettuce followed the orange.

Sophie opened her mouth to let out a scream of frustration—but, of course, she didn't. As a little girl, she'd been the attention-grabbing drama princess of the family, but at twenty-eight, she'd long conquered those nuisance traits. She could stay steady and calm in a tornado. Everyone said so.

The trick, of course, was simply self-discipline. She ignored the lost orange and lettuce, the same way she ignored the rain dripping from her eyelashes and the squish of water in her shoes. Her arms and shoulders were trying to fall off, groaning from the combined weight of the groceries, her purse, her laptop and her briefcase of references—but she'd carried heavier than this on the trek home from the metro, and she would again. She was mighty. She was strong.

Sometimes.

She forged ahead the next half block, reminding herself of all the reasons she'd loved living in Foggy Bottom these last nine months. She *loved* her current work project. She was crazy about the old brownstone apartment. She loved the urban neighborhood—how easy it had been to find other young professional people and make friends. She loved having access to such a super metro system that she didn't need a car. She loved…

The soggy grocery sack suddenly split. It didn't completely crack open, just tore several inches, but that was enough to send more groceries spilling down the street. Again, Sophie was tempted to let out a good, bellowing yell. Instead, she ran.

Six more houses. Then five. The sleazy-cold rain had already soaked her blond head, slivered down her neck. Four houses. She could see hers ahead—the old brown brick with white shutters, the wrought-iron fence circling a yard the size of a closet, the broken steps up to the elegant old front door.

Her foot stumbled on a sidewalk crack. Her armload

threatened to tumble completely. She ran faster, praying now. Three houses. Two. She prayed to God. To Buddha. To Mother Nature. To anyone who could help her just move those last few steps, inside to shelter.

One house away, then *home*. Up the three steps. Belatedly, she realized that the key was buried inside her purse—which she couldn't possibly get to, not without dropping everything. But then she discovered that just possibly there was a God, because the front door was open.

Well, it wasn't exactly wide open, but the door was definitely ajar—ajar enough for her to burst through, gasping for breath, dripping rain like a drenched puppy.

Just inside, a small antique chandelier lit the vestibule with the effectiveness of a candle in the wind. Still, it wasn't the dimness that made Sophie suddenly stumble. For some crazy reason, a big bulky object blocked the entrance, right inside the door.

Disaster was instantaneous. Her overfilled grocery bag split completely. Milk and Tampax and cereal and tomatoes and oranges went flying. Then she did. Knowing a crash was inevitable, she reacted instinctively to protect her laptop and precious research, but she landed so hard on her right hip and elbow that she saw stars—outraged, blinding, dizzying stars. Whoever left the monster-size thing on the floor was going to get a piece of her mind, the very second she…

One twist of her head, and she saw the body.

It wasn't a thing on the floor.

It was a body. A bare-naked body. Her hunk of a neighbor's body.

Shock seemed to turn her to stone. She couldn't move,

couldn't breathe, couldn't think. There wasn't a sound in the place, not the creak of a floorboard, nothing to indicate anyone was around. And of course there wasn't. The larger downstairs apartment had been vacant for over a month now, and upstairs, there were only two apartments—hers and Jon Pruitt's.

Jon… She couldn't look at him, couldn't *not* look at him, but suddenly her heart stopped beating in big, panicked thumps. Jon was the womanizer of the universe, the heartthrob of every woman in the neighborhood, and the selfish son of a sea dog who neglected his cat. Sophie had as much in common with him as a bunny had with a shark, but damn. He'd been decent to her. They'd turned into amazingly compatible neighbors.

This had to be a nightmare. A terrible dream.

Yet oxygen scrabbled into her lungs when she spotted the nail-polish-red gleaming under his head. That red was real, no dream, and the look of it propelled her into action. She hurtled over all the debris on the floor and crouched down to press on the pulse in his neck—just in case all that glossy red color was misleading. Just in case there was a chance he was still alive.

No.

His skin was cold. Blank eyes stared up at her.

*Wake up, Sophie. Wake up, and for God's sake, don't hurl.*

She pushed back, landing on her rump, her fingertips suddenly icy and her stomach clenching with horror.

Suddenly Sophie was five years old again—and of course, she knew that was stupid. This shock had no remote connection to her past. The new trauma just seemed to trigger the old one. It was the same old flash flood of a mental slide show, the images darting through her brain, her in a long yellow nightgown, her cold feet stinging in the wet grass, the darkness, the stinky smoke and sharp flames, her mom screaming, screaming, her clutching her sisters, the three of them wailing, then the firemen carrying both those stretchers out....

Sophie sucked in a lungful of air, then another. Letting those train-wreck memories out was always a mistake. Obviously, she'd never forgotten the fire. The grief and trauma still flavored every nightmare and always would. No one could just forget anything that devastating. But that old loss and grief and terror weren't the problem right now.

*Get a grip, Sophie.*

She struggled to. Obviously, this wasn't about her, but about Jon. This was no time to be thinking about herself. She swallowed the swell of nausea and whipped around for her purse. Naturally, it was chock-full of everything she'd need to survive living in Europe for six months. She rummaged, rummaged, until she finally located her cell phone. It took three tries for her fumbling fingers to accurately dial 911.

Then she just huddled against the far corner wall and shook, waiting for the police.

Cord Pruitt saw the lecture doors open, but initially paid no attention. It wouldn't be the first time a student popped in late. His Thursday-night class on International Studies was invariably stuffed to the gills—which always tickled his sense of irony.

Ten years ago, he'd have sworn he would rather be a snake handler than teach. He'd meant it. But when family problems forced him back to Washington a few years ago, Georgetown had taken one look at his background in languages and Foreign Service and offered him a job. In spite of all odds, the university monsters had grown on him. The kids were all motivated, bright, the type who gave a serious damn. Hell, they even stayed awake during his lectures.

Temporarily, the decibel level rivaled a rowdy bar. The topic of debate was the relationship between religion and poverty in various cultures, and whether religion or poverty was the strongest political influence. The subject definitely wouldn't turn on everyone, but his kids were raucously enthused.

Maybe a little too raucously.

"Okay, okay, settle down for two shakes," he interjected. "I'm hearing too many opinions, and not enough facts to back them up. Give me stats, people. I want numbers. I want proof. You're starting to sound like the media, instead of people with a brain."

That brought a laugh...but they readily knuckled down to a good verbal fight again.

The next time Cord glanced up, he noted the lecture doors were still gaping open, with two men—two grown men, definitely not students—standing in the doorway. They didn't interrupt, didn't speak, didn't intrude. They were just lodged in the entranceway like a pair of rocks.

Cord's pulse bucked uneasily. Years of Foreign Service had honed his ability to size up both people and problems. One of the men was gray haired, sharp faced and sharp eyed, with a wiry, lean build. Cord figured him for a private cop. The other guy looked younger, more like forty, with paunchy eyes and the habitual tired expression of a detective.

This close to D.C., private and public cops were as

common as ants. Still, Cord couldn't imagine why one would be here, in his classroom—much less why the ferret and hound would be paired together.

"All right. Let's wrap this up," Cord said, but he didn't really want to wrap up the class at all. It was twenty minutes to ten. Outside, it was a bone-chilling, rainy night, but inside, Cord had been perfectly happy, his boots up on the desk, his arms cocked behind his neck, occasionally stirring himself to referee the debate...but the two strangers made it impossible to concentrate.

He couldn't imagine what they wanted...but it couldn't be good. Cord was fatalistic about bad luck. It never showed up when you were in the mood, because you were never in the mood.

"Okay, I know you think you escaped a bullet by getting out early, but don't start thinking I'm going easy on you. Next Tuesday night, I just might keep you until after eleven."

This threat was greeted with mixed laughter and groans. Students rustled into their jackets, stood up, dropped books, made all the usual noise it took to scoot them out of the place. Even on a medieval dark night like this one, they were more revved than tired, and damn it, when Cord finally got them charged up about ideas and thinking and bigger worlds, he hated to let them go.

The place had completely cleared out before the two strangers headed down the aisle. Cord had stood up by then, was pushing papers and books into his folio, reaching for his old alpaca jacket...but he watched them.

"Cord Pruitt?"

Cord nodded. Both men showed their IDs. As expected, the jowly, tired-looking guy was a detective,

George Bassett. The other man—the more interesting character with the long, sharp features—was private security. Ian Ferrell had a tag from the Senate Office Building, so, pretty obviously, he was on some senator's staff. Cord was even more mystified why they'd be paired together.

"I'm afraid we're here about your brother, sir." Bassett's tone was respectful.

"Jon?" Okay, dumb question. It wasn't as if he had any other brother. But his muscles were freezing up now, anticipating a blow.

"Yes, sir. I'm afraid we have bad news. Perhaps you might want to sit down."

Cord pushed off his jacket, but there was no way he was sitting down. "You can skip the tact and cushioning with me. Just tell me what kind of trouble he's in now."

The men exchanged glances, but the detective picked up the ball. "We received a 911 call late this afternoon. When officers responded to the scene, we found a man lying at the bottom of the stairs. He was deceased. I'm sorry for your loss, sir—"

That had been tacked on as if the detective had suddenly forgotten his usual lines in a play.

Cord sagged against the desk. There was no love lost between him and Jon. Years ago he'd stopped believing his brother would find an ethic or principle in his character.

But five tons of flash-flood memories suddenly seared through his mind. Cord had been roaming the world for God knew how many years now. He'd still likely be hightailing it from Everest to the Amazon, from Delphi to Paris to Rio...if their mother hadn't come down with cancer. By the time he'd severed his work ties and got back to Washington, it was too late. Mom was gone. Dad had crashed and had to be put in what they discreetly called a rehab center. Over the last years, Jon had turned into someone Cord couldn't even recognize, much less reach. And Zoe had left him, because coming home to clean up family messes wasn't exactly her specialty.

More fool Cord. He'd actually thought she was the kind of woman who'd stand by him.

His brother, on the other hand, had always been trouble. Cord could readily believe Jon had promoted himself to even bigger trouble—but still, nothing like this. Not dead. Not murdered.

Cord swiped a hand over his face, tried to surface from the weight of shock. And guilt.

"Where's my brother now?" Cord asked hoarsely. "Who did this? What—?"

The detective quietly interrupted. "It took us a few hours to track you down. Initially, we assumed your father was the primary family connection, but then we realized..."

"That he's in a rest home."

"Yes. So from there, we tried to ascertain if your brother had any other direct relatives—which is how we came across your name. Obviously, you weren't at your home address, so we tracked you down through the university, and then where you'd be lecturing at this hour—all of which is to say, this all took time. It has been a few hours since the event. Initially we weren't certain if your brother fell down the stairs or if there could have been foul play—"

Impatiently, Cord pushed away from the desk. Bassett was talking a lot, but saying very little, arousing Cord's worry buttons even more. Obviously, his brother hadn't had an accidental fall. And obviously, even a murder must have had unusually complicated implications, or these two men would never have shown up together.

"What do you need from me?" he asked curtly, addressing the private cop rather than the detective. The man had been silent all this time, but Cord sensed he was the higher authority of the two.

"Mr. Pruitt...the situation is complex."

Cord had already guessed that. Situations involving Jon were always complicated. He rubbed the back of his neck, trying to fathom how his dad was going to survive this.

"Are you familiar with a young woman named Sophie Campbell?"

"No," Cord said.

"She's the tenant who lived next door to your brother—from the time she moved here, somewhere around nine months ago. She's the person who found him. She apparently knew your brother quite well."

Cord sighed. "So did a lot of women."

Bullets kept shooting through his mind. Funeral arrangements had to be made. Someone had to deal with his brother's business, from bills to belongings. Their father was hooked up to oxygen full-time, wouldn't be able to handle anything—just telling him would be a crisis in itself—and thank God they'd lost their mother, because she'd have crumpled to find out what Jon had become and how he'd died.

"Who did this? Do you know?" Cord asked again.

"That's exactly what we need your help with."

Cord wanted to throw something. Too many people

could have wanted to strangle his brother. Himself included.

He paced around the desk, stared at the black diamonds sluicing down the windows, the pitch-black night, the bleakness of it. "Look. I can't seem to grasp any of this. You think this woman, this Campbell person, killed him? Is that why you mentioned her?"

They all pulled back for a moment. Neither man had moved from their rock-quiet position in front of him. The detective, Bassett, started to say, "At this time, this soon, there's no possibility of our knowing anything definitively—"

But Ferrell interrupted him, looked directly into Cord's eyes. "Your brother has been under private investigation for the last two months. I believe he's been blackmailing two women, and possibly more. He had a pattern of targeting high-profile women, where a public scandal would have crippled their lives. My client is a senator, but believe me, she isn't the only one who wants this matter handled as privately as possible."

"We absolutely want to find out who murdered your brother," Bassett clipped in.

"But we also want access to the blackmail evidence your brother had. It's no one's goal to impede the investigation. Everyone concerned wants the killer brought to light. But in an ideal world, the innocent victims wouldn't be exposed to a media circus."

"Holy hell." Cord rubbed the back of his neck again.

"We have no absolute evidence of blackmail—" the detective interjected, but Ferrell interrupted him again, his voice quiet and sure.

"No one expected your brother's death. No one knew

for sure how far your brother's…activities…had gone, or how many women were involved. But right now it's a tangled mess. A lot of people could be hurt if this is handled the wrong way."

Cord wished his thermos wasn't empty. His throat was dryer than the Sahara. They kept heaping on more bad news. "Maybe we'd better get a few things straight before you say any more," he told both men. "I did a stint in the Air Force, donated some years to the State Department—easy enough for you to check my background, and I'm guessing you already have. But being a patriot doesn't mean I have any use for politics and politicians. I don't. I don't spy and I don't lie. So if that's what you're asking me—"

"It's not, Mr. Pruitt. But we are asking for your discretion, and your help. We absolutely want to bring whoever did this to justice. But we believe that it's in everyone's best interests to keep this under the media radar as much as possible—"

Bassett was long-winded and careful. Ferrell cut to the chase. "It's too soon to draw conclusions. We all know that. But as an initial strategy, it makes good sense to publicize your brother's death as an accidental fall. Temporarily, not forever. There's no question, at least in my mind, that this was a murder—"

"Although we won't know that until the results of an autopsy. We know very few specifics this soon."

Ferrell rolled his eyes. "It was murder," he repeated to Cord. "But the reason we want the media calling it accidental is to gain an advantage. The murderer wouldn't be on her guard."

"We don't positively know that it's a 'her,'" the detective piped up again, but Ferrell ignored him.

"If the murderer feels safe, she could slip, make mistakes. The women involved with your brother are going to want that blackmail evidence, Mr. Pruitt. There are pictures, notes, CDs. We know that, but we don't know where they are. We believe the murderer—as well as the other women involved in your brother's life—will likely take some major risks to find that evidence. To destroy it."

The detective took his turn. "Your brother's next-door neighbor," he said, "is twenty-eight…"

"That's the Sophie Campbell you mentioned?" Cord asked.

"Yes. She works as a translator for Open World. She's been with that organization since she graduated from college. She does extensive translating projects for them, often on-site. For the last nine months or so, she's been living in Foggy Bottom, gathering stories from women survivors in World War II. She speaks Russian, German, Danish."

Cord's head was swimming. "I don't understand why you keep bringing up this woman—unless you either believe she was one of the women Jon was blackmailing, or that she's the killer."

"We don't know either of those things," Ferrell said. "But we do believe she's the key to your brother's killer in some way."

"Why?"

"We're not really at liberty to say," the detective said cautiously, but again, the private cop proved more frank.

"We're uncertain to what extent this young woman is involved. What we do know, however, is that she was the only consistent person in your brother's life. She was in and out of your brother's place quite frequently. In fact, she's the only one who had a key, as far as we know." The older man hunched closer. "We need your help, Mr. Pruitt. We need your help to solve this…and we need your discretion."

Cord frowned. "I still don't know what you're asking me to do. If you need my permission to go through Jon's place, fine, you've got it. I assume you'd have that legal right, regardless, in a crime situation—"

"It's not that simple. What we also need is you, specifically because you're his brother, a family member. Once we've officially—so to speak—labeled this an accidental death, we need you to go in, act like a grieving brother, look like you're closing up Jon's affairs."

"That's hardly going to be an act," Cord said. "It's what I have to do. There is no one else."

"Exactly. The thing is, wherever your brother hid his stockpile of information, he hid it well. It's not as if we haven't been trying to track down evidence long before this happened. And although we don't know precisely what role Sophie Campbell plays in this, we *do* know she had more access to his place, to him, than anyone else. We haven't been able to dig up any incriminating background on her, but we all believe she knows more than she's saying. Someone who wasn't connected to the law might have a significantly better chance to get her talking."

Cord grabbed his jacket and folio of student papers and notes. Enough was enough. He'd had more than he could take. "If you're asking me to spy, as I said before—forget it."

"We're asking you to talk to her. Which should naturally happen if you're in your brother's apartment—she's right there. If she happens to tell you information that you judge as valuable, we're asking you to communicate—preferably to me, first." This, from the detective.

But it was Ferrell who was looking at him. Ferrell who wanted anything he dug up. *First.*

Cord motioned them all to the door. This party was over. He wished he could hurl something. Even though he was two years younger than Jon, he couldn't remember a time he wasn't cleaning up Jon's messes... but this was by far the most disturbing and ugliest.

As far as this Sophie character, though, Cord already had her pictured, because he knew the kind of woman his brother went for.

Jon liked sluts. Lookers with long legs and spongy morals. Often enough, Jon pursued women who were married or already committed, because he found it more fun to seduce a woman who was supposed to be faithful. His favorite types had money, or looked as if they did. He preferred long-haired brunettes who had that look at a party—like they were prowling the gathering for men, like a cat hunted for meat.

Not that Cord minded wildcats.

He'd even tamed a few in the past. But at the moment, he was off women altogether—the hurt from Zoe still stuck like a blade—and beyond that, any woman who appealed to his brother never could, never would, ring his chimes.

"You'll help us?" Bassett pressed again.

"Maybe." Cord couldn't think anymore. Not right now. "I need to get my brother buried. I need to deal with my father. I need to find out what I'm supposed to do as executor, and all that nonsense. I assume you don't want me near the place until you've done whatever investigating you plan to do. So give me the word when I've got the freedom to go in, handle the place and my brother's things. I'll be happy to give you anything relevant I run across."

Ferrell looked as if he could finally breathe. "That's all we're asking."

Cord shot him a dry look. "Right."

When he'd finally ushered the two men out the door, he stood in the lecture hall a moment longer. Rain was still drizzling down the windows, highlighting the loneliness of yellow lamplight on scarred desks. Out of nowhere, he felt the crushing weight of grief. He and Jon had always been polar opposites, but damn…

Maybe there'd never been respect or even liking. But they had been brothers.

He'd do what he could.

He just dreaded the days ahead.

# Chapter 2

"You know how much I love Caviar...." Sophie had been bubbling on for the last few minutes, but her voice faltered when she reached the apartment door. Even days later, it was hard to open that door, hard to step into the front hall without reliving the vision of Jon's body lying there.

Thankfully, the Sunday coffee klatch group had insisted on walking her home. Now the three women all crowded into the cramped hall, no one planning on staying, just keeping her company for a few more minutes.

They weren't just supporting her, Sophie knew. Jon's death had the whole neighborhood in morbid thrall—especially the women. Crime wasn't new in D.C., but this was someone they knew. Every female in a three-mile radius—except Sophie—had lusted after Jon.

Quite a few had sampled his sexual talents—or so they claimed.

"Don't start about that Caviar business, Sophie." Jan Howell was the tallest of the three brunettes, the trust funder who loved a party, artsy clothes and anything to do with gossip. Still, she had a good heart, and automatically started handing over the debris Sophie had dropped on the walk—her fuzzy gray scarf, her mitten, her half-eaten muffin in a bag. "You'd take in every stray critter in the city, if we let you."

"Not *every* one," Sophie said, defending herself. When the women laughed, she tried a different defense, since they obviously weren't buying that one. "The thing is, I really do love Caviar. And right now, it's such a relief to have him. I come home from work and it's so silent in here. At least I can curl up on the couch with *some* kind of warm body...."

Again, her voice trailed off.

Damn, but she couldn't seem to stop reliving it. That night. The cops. The detective with the cheap coat and hound-dog eyes, hunkering over her, asking her slow, patient questions. Her, blurting out that she had to find Caviar. Him, acting like she was a rich, spoiled—and suspicious—fruitcake. The flashing lights and lobby full of strangers and then that horrible silence after they all left and she was alone, with a rotten case of the jitters.

"You called your sisters, didn't you?" Hillary Smythe looked more like a bar waitress than a doctor. Shiny dark curls stretched down her back, accenting gorgeous skin and boobs that tended to exuberantly burst out of anything she wore. For the next year, she was studying under some fancy gene research doc at GW University, just a few blocks away. Sophie had long wondered if

Hillary had some troubling secret in her past, because she was always so quiet—but she never missed a Sunday-morning coffee with the rest.

"I called both sisters the day after it happened," Sophie assured her. "I almost wish I hadn't. They've been calling nonstop ever since. Sooner or later, I'll get a tougher skin about this. It's just...right now I still have that image of Jon every time I walk in the door."

"Well, of course you do. It was a god-awful thing to go through!"

Penelope Martin leaned against the thin row of mailboxes. She was stare-at beautiful, Sophie'd always thought. Breathtaking eyes, fabulous figure, dark hair rich and lustrous. The others sometimes whispered that she was harder than nails—Sophie could see she was a little manipulative, but she always stuck up for her. Penelope worked as a lobbyist, after all, and you just couldn't be cupcake-sweet and do that kind of job. More than the others, though, Penelope was enthralled with "the Jon situation," as she called it. "I just can't believe that the police decided it was an accidental death instead of murder. I mean, from how you described it, Sophie—"

Sophie unzipped her jacket and sank down on the third step. "Well, they seemed to decide that he was naked because he'd probably been taking a shower. And then maybe he ran downstairs for his mail, thinking no one was there. I'm the only other tenant in the building right now, and Jon knew I rarely get home before five."

"Actually, that sounds logical to me." Jan invariably took the authoritative voice in these conversations, because she was the only one in the group who claimed to have nailed Jon—not that Hillary and Penelope hadn't tried.

Jon would undoubtedly have fit them all in, if he'd lived long enough. With the exception of Sophie, of course. No one believed Jon would ever have come on to Sophie. Including Sophie.

Jan was still immersed in speculations. "Heaven knows, I can picture Jon running around naked without a qualm. He didn't have a modest bone in his body. But it was freezing and rainy that afternoon. Logically, I'd have thought he'd have pulled on a jacket or something, even if he was only running downstairs for the mail."

"Well, maybe it wasn't for mail. Maybe it was a delivery. UPS, or something like that."

"But there was no package," Hillary reminded them all—she who could always be counted on to remember details. "Besides, Sophie said he didn't have a mailbox key on him."

"He literally didn't have anything on him," Sophie affirmed.

Penelope backtracked to her primary area of interest. "So...was he as hung as all the women said? Oh, that's right, Jan, you already knew firsthand—"

"God, what a thing to bring up."

Penelope let out a bark of a laugh. "*Up* is *definitely* the relevant word. I heard that when a man dies, he tends to be erect. True or not, Sophie? You're the only one who'd know."

Sophie rolled her eyes. "You're horrible! All of you!" But they weren't horrible. They'd stayed long enough to make sure she was okay, even though she knew perfectly well they had stuff to do. "Thanks so much, everybody, for walking me in. I'm better, I swear. In fact, I'm going straight upstairs to curl up on the couch with my big guy."

"That's our Sophie. Always the wild one," Hillary said, teasing, but then she said, more thoughtfully, "But that's really the point about Jon. Why his accidentally dying just seems so ironic. I mean, he *was* wild. You'd think a number of the women he dropped would have been happy to kill him."

"Happy to sleep with him, you mean," Jan said dryly. "I'll bet it was half the D.C. area. The only women wanting to kill him would be those under the insane misconception he might grow up and consider a serious commitment."

"Well..." Penelope still wasn't ready to let it go. "At least no one ever complained he didn't show a woman a good time. He just couldn't stick to one woman."

"Except for Sophie, of course," Hillary teased.

"Hey. No need to bring me into this discussion."

"Well, you *are* the only woman who escaped being ensnared by Jon, that we all know of. Cripes, I'd have settled for being hurt. I never got a chance to make a play." Penelope sounded increasingly mournful.

"Well, speaking for myself, I'm happier with Caviar. I'll take my bodies rich and soft. Something to keep you warm at night and make no demands. In fact—"

Penelope suddenly let out a screech worthy of a cat in heat. "Oh! Oh my God, you scared me half to death!"

"I'm sorry."

The front hall only had space for two bodies at the best of times, and temporarily there were three stuffed in there. Sophie was out of the way, sitting on the carpeted step, but she was just as startled by the sudden sound of a distinctly masculine voice. Sophie twisted, trying to catch a glimpse of the intruder from around Hillary's elbow...and then froze in shock.

For an instant, she thought the man in the doorway was Jon.

Sophie had long accepted that she was doomed to have more bonkers moments than most, but believing in ghosts was still a stretch.

Yet even after a second glance, she still thought he was Jon.

She yanked off her glasses and squinted seriously now. Jon had unquestionably been a prize-winning scoundrel, but there'd never been any surprise how he attracted women. First off, he stretched to a good six two or three. Add in shoulders made for a tux, posture with a little arrogance and the most compelling blue eyes ever made. Then stir in the tasty stuff.

Jon's face would have been Adonis-perfect, if not for the French nose, but his skin was Irish-clear, the hair a Nordic dark blond. His eyebrows had a hint of an Italian slant, the chin and bones a Germanic tough cut. And no, Jon couldn't possibly have all those heritages, but that was the point. He was a universal hunk. Take all the parts, and the whole appealed to any and every woman's fantasy...except for hers, of course. Sophie figured she was the only woman who ever felt completely safe around him, because there wasn't a prayer in the universe he'd notice her. Not *that* way.

Now, though, her heart finally stopped hammering. The longer she scrutinized the intruder in the doorway, the more she realized this was no ghost.

He did look like Jon—amazingly like Jon—but there were interesting differences. This guy's hair was blond, but darker than Jon's, more whiskey-gold, all wind-riled-up, and longish. His legs were encased in cords—Jon never wore that nature of casual pants—and these were well-worn cords besides. The chin was scruffy, where Jon never left the house without fresh-shaved cheeks and an expensive aftershave.

And Jon had never once made her pulse bounce like a hormonal puppy…yet this man did. Sophie ignored the tickle of awareness, because she was obviously having a highly emotional week, and her judgment couldn't be trusted.

While Sophie was giving herself a mental slap upside the head, though, the other women were sizing him up as if they'd just discovered a sale at Bloomingdale's.

The man was looking over the women just as sharply and intensely. His gaze roamed from one to the other like a bee checking out pollen—except for her. He spotted her sitting on the steps. His attention just immediately passed by her. No surprise there.

All three brunettes were gorgeous, but even besides that, Sophie knew men never noticed her. It was the same reason she'd been safe as a church with Jon. A woman didn't wear oversize coats and big bags and gloppy hats for nothing. Sophie knew perfectly well she was ignorable.

Her neighbors, however, didn't have the same life goal of being safe.

"You don't live here." Penelope surged past Hillary's purse and Jan's boots to extend a hand. "Not that you aren't welcome." She gave him a head-to-toe, at the same time he took in her red wool jacket, matching red lip gloss and flip-back brunette hair.

He accepted the handshake. "I'm Cord Pruitt. Jon Pruitt's brother."

"Oh. *Oh.*" Sophie almost laughed as Penelope's expression changed channels from woman on the hunt to sweetie pie. Suddenly, her eyes were brimming with sympathy. "We were just talking about how much we all loved your brother and missed him. It's been such a shock—"

Sophie relaxed another notch, now that his identity had been established. For some strange reason, though, he seemed to instantly lose interest in Penelope's considerable charms—and moved on to Hillary.

Hillary, usually so quiet, seemed to perk up under the stranger's attention. "Hi. I'm Hillary Smythe. I'm a doctor, on a research sabbatical at George Washington U. I met your brother almost the first week I moved here. We talked quite often. You must be the brother who's the ultra brain?"

Sophie was amazed. Apparently, a terrific-looking man could coax Hillary out of her normally quiet mode.

"Thanks, both of you," Cord said to the first two who'd introduced themselves. "I appreciate the chance to meet people who knew Jon. I hope you can find some time to tell me more, sometime over the next few weeks. I have to say, his death was a real shock."

He had one of those sexy Josh Groban voices, Sophie realized, so it was perfectly natural that she couldn't think straight. Any female old enough to walk would be mesmerized by that voice. Again, though, she noticed his attention zoomed past Hillary, and suddenly settled with dazzling concentration on Penelope.

"You *must* be Sophie," he said to Penelope. "So you're the one who lived across the hall from my brother—"

Sophie was startled to hear her name—even more

startled to see how fast he'd forgotten Hillary. No man in his right mind forgot Hillary.

She might be a little quiet, but she was both brilliant and stunning.

Since Cord had specifically spoken her name, though, she felt an obligation to pipe up, "I'm Sophie. And yes, I live upstairs, across from your brother."

Penelope's jaw dropped. She was clearly astonished to be passed over, and undoubtedly thought the grief-stricken man had made a mistake, because she homed in in front of Cord faster than a GPS. "And I'm Penelope Martin. I was friends with your brother, too. We all live within a few blocks of each other. You know how Foggy Bottom is. Jon and I loved to talk about the political scene after work on Fridays...and a bunch of us would have coffee early mornings at The Beanery, just down the street—"

Sophie wondered whether Cord needed glasses. Or bifocals. He completely ignored Penelope, too, almost pushing Pen aside to squint down. "*You're* Sophie?"

Sophie could smell an insult from a hundred paces. She just couldn't figure out what the insult was, exactly. For unknown reasons, he seemed surprised to identify her. Shocked, even.

Before she had a chance to respond, he echoed, "You're *sure* you're Sophie?"

As if she wouldn't know who she was? She cocked a fuzzy-gloved hand under her chin. "Oh, yeah, I'm reasonably sure. And now I can see the family resemblance between you and Jon."

Now he got the insulted look. Even though he couldn't possibly know what the insult was, exactly.

Close up, Sophie's hormones not only perked up, but

suddenly stood at military attention. He didn't just look like Jon. He was about a thousand, million times sexier than Jon. On a scale of one to ten, he scored somewhere around four hundred.

My God, those eyes.

That mouth.

That butt.

Not that his sexiness was relevant to anything.

But at least, for the first time in days, she wasn't thinking about dead, naked bodies.

# *Chapter 3*

Cord stomped up the stairs behind that tight little butt, well aware he'd completely failed to charm Ms. Sophie Campbell, but hell, he was expecting a looker. A brunette, buxom looker, definitely not a blond, much less a flyaway blond with stick-up cowlicks, an oversize jacket and fresh pink cheeks like a country girl.

Cord kept wanting to shake his head. Obviously, a player came in all sizes and shapes. Honest eyes and baby-soft skin were no measure of character.

It was just really, really challenging to imagine his brother with Sophie—not just as a blackmailing cohort, but as a sexual interest. Particularly when the whole neighborhood seemed crammed with exceptionally attractive brunettes who were everything Jon ever panted after.

"Mr. Pruitt...Cord...you might have heard me say I loved Caviar."

Yeah, he'd heard a bunch of the women's chitchat. Initially he hadn't even seen Sophie, because she was hidden on the stair steps. But he'd heard the other woman identify her, and directly heard that butter-soft voice talking about loving caviar and tomcats and how she preferred her bodies "rich and soft."

Cord wasn't passing judgments. He was just hearing exactly what he expected from one of his brother's sex partners—a shallow, all-about-me personality, with liquid morals. It wasn't just his opinion, for Pete's sake. Those were the same personality flaws that made the cops, private and public, believe Sophie was part of his brother's blackmail schemes...and was likely directly involved in Jon's murder.

Only, now that he'd seen her, he couldn't believe it. The soft blue eyes showed no sign of guile. The outfit was as attractive as a potato sack. She dropped one of her multicolored mittens on the fifth step—they looked like something a kid would wear.

He picked it up. The second mitten slipped out of her jacket pocket somewhere around the tenth step. He picked that up, too.

Then she dropped a book.

Then her scarf pooled on the floor when she rummaged at the top of the stairs for her apartment key.

Cord thought her performance was Academy Award winning. Who would ever guess that she was a mercenary, manipulative bitch? Anyone would be fooled into thinking she was an absentminded, sweet soul without a greedy bone in her entire body.

"Cord." She repeated his name again, and then took a big, brave breath—as if he were falling for this act.

"I realize you have a right to your brother's things. Totally. But I honestly don't think it's a fair thing to do, to take Caviar. It's not about ownership. It's about love. I spent more time with him than Jon ever did. So I'm just asking if you'd consider letting me keep him. Or at least, if you'd give me a chance to show how happy he is with me."

"Huh?"

She opened her door about the same time Cord unlocked his brother's. Light flowed from windows in both flats. His brother's place—Cord only glanced for a millisecond—looked like a gadget-lover's techno paradise.

Hers looked like a fire sale for ruffles.

She peered up at him, waving a hand. "Are you awake?"

He didn't bat her hand away, but he was as annoyed as…well, as if she were a pesky little sister. "Of course I'm awake. I just didn't understand your question."

"The cat… *This* cat…is Caviar."

"Caviar," he echoed, as the lightbulb finally dawned. She'd been referring not to the expensive salty stuff you put on crackers, but to a cat.

And not just any cat. The scrawny, skinny, ugly, huge-boned feline hurled toward Sophie the instant she unlocked the door. It was a motley blend of black and white and orange, all run together like spilled paint. It wound around Sophie's legs like a fuzzy snake, purring louder than thunder.

Sophie crouched down to pet it, dropping everything in her wake—purse, mittens, hat, book and all. Even the first stroke made the cat's purr rise another decibel level.

"Your brother, as I'm sure you know, was no animal lover. Caviar just showed up one day and refused to leave. Jon opened the door and the cat just shot in and hid, couldn't be found. Jon fed it, but every time he tried to put the cat outside, Caviar would find another hiding place, until Jon finally gave up. Anyway, whenever Jon was going to be gone overnight—which was a *lot* of nights—he'd put a note on my door so I'd feed Caviar. Or take him in with me."

This thrilling story almost put Cord to sleep. He had stuff to do. All of it unsettling, none of it pleasant. And yeah, he hadn't forgotten the cops wanted him to grill Sophie. In his life, he'd done plenty of tough things, but so far, that never included kicking a puppy.

She seemed to think he was hesitating because he wanted the cat himself. "Look," she said. "Just come in for a minute. Have a cup of coffee or tea. You'll see what Caviar is like, how he is with me. And maybe I can help you with some of your brother's things. I don't know what you might need, but…"

Hell. Maybe he'd misjudged the puppy thing. The cops had sure led him to expect she'd offer some way to get into Jon's stuff. And like it or not, Cord couldn't see how he could turn down the chance to find out more information.

He took a step inside her place, wary as a fox in coyote territory.

Besides the ruffles all over the curtains and pillows and all, she seemed to decorate in old furniture and messes. A hanging birdcage held a giant fern. Open magazines and books blanketed a coffee table, and the floor, and a chair or two. A window seat had been covered with somewhere around thirty pillows. The couch looked saggy, the kind of couch that swallowed up a body and never let it out again. The wallpaper was flowers, the couch cover was flowers and the jammed bookcases, spilling over with books, had vases of flowers on top of them.

Cord felt momentarily light-headed. It was close to a toxic dose of estrogen. Two martinis on an empty stomach didn't pack this much of a wallop.

"Cream or sugar in your coffee?" She showed up in the far doorway.

"Just black. But you don't have to..."

She disappeared before he'd finished refusing the coffee. Cord reminded himself that he was a proven tough guy, a Marine with honors, an athlete who'd come damn close to an Olympic win, a man who'd survived some impossible challenges in his overseas project years. But he was afraid to take off his coat.

She was one scary cookie.

He wound his way around the clutter slowly, and then parked in the kitchen doorway. It wasn't much of a kitchen. Typical of an old house, the woodwork had been painted a hundred times. The walls were sun-yellow, plants stealing what little counter space she had, and the appliances dated back to the dark ages. A computer and books and heaps of paper covered the entire surface of the kitchen table, so it was a cinch she didn't try eating there.

"I take it this is your desk."

"Yeah, no choice, there is no other place. Now, I know this looks bad. It's not like I want cat hair near the food." She motioned with her head toward the cat, who was perched on the counter like a god overlooking his realm. Sophie handed Cord a mug, took one for herself. "Caviar was always a little like your brother. He's so good, if you just let him do what he wants. And it's not as if there's a point in arguing with him, because he's not going to listen to you anyway."

"You knew my brother pretty well."

"In certain ways, yes." There was something in her voice. A message, but he couldn't read it.

She led him back to the living room, shunted papers and magazines aside to give him a seat. The cat followed them in, perched on the high edge of the sofa, clearly determined to chaperone the pair.

Although, how the word *chaperone* popped into Cord's mind, he had no idea.

"You work at home?" he asked her.

"I've worked in Italy, Peacock, Georgia, the Isle of Man, Luray, Virginia…and I'd probably work in a ditch, if that's where Open World sent me—that's the name of the company I work for. Right now, I'm doing a long-term translating project, and I should be in Foggy Bottom for over a year. Although I hope they find more projects here after that, because I'd like to settle down. The traveling's fun, seeing new places, experiencing new cultures, but I'm just really sick of renting. I'd like to have a home base."

She'd spilled more information than he'd asked—times ten. A chatterbox would hardly seem a common character trait in a woman who had a ton to hide. Cord found himself intrigued. Not that he was about to tell her about his State Department or service background, but he was definitely startled to hear more about her background. Who'd guess they had any similarities?

"So, what's the long-term translating project you're working on?"

"It's really pretty fascinating. I'm interviewing women who survived WWII. European women who lived in countries directly affected by Hitler's domination back then. Eventually, all the stories will come together into an intensive research project. Anyway, 'my' ladies are a Russian, a German woman, and my first was a Danish lady. I just finished her story. It was fascinating. She was only nine when the U.S. joined the war. She remembers her dad, a sailor, fishing our American pilots out of the sea, night after night. Everyone hid the American soldiers—in fruit cellars, under beds, wherever they could. She remembers..." Sophie suddenly laughed. "I know, I know, I can go on all night. I can't help it. I love my job. But you don't want to hear all this."

Confounding him completely was that he did. Want to hear more. Maybe her ditsiness was contagious. "It sounds interesting," he said stiffly, "but actually, right now—"

She finished his sentence for him. "You have much more serious things on your mind." She'd just perched on a chair arm and now bounced up again. "I almost forgot. I've got piles of your brother's mail for you. I don't know what the authorities did with Jon's mail when they were investigating. But once they stopped coming... well, the box got overstuffed almost right away, and I had the key to Jon's box, so I just started bringing it in. I'd done it for him before. I knew someone would come sooner or later about the apartment, all his things." She hesitated. "You're going to need some help."

"You sound sure of that."

Whatever she answered, Cord missed. He wasn't used

to feeling thrown off balance, but she was sure as hell doing it to him. Nothing about her was what he'd been led to expect—particularly once he saw her moving around with her jacket off.

She was still wearing clothes that would work on a nun's runway. Baggy blue sweater, hanging way past her hips. Skinny jeans. Sloppy socks. Her blond hair was clipped out of the way, wisping all over the place. But…when she walked, when she moved, he could see there were no extra pounds under the sweater.

She had a slim waist. Serious breasts—not huge, not blatant, but she couldn't totally conceal a downright arresting figure, even under those clothes. The legs weren't long—she was shorter than a shrimp—but the proportions were right. And maybe she wasn't into face paint and all, but her skin was irresistibly soft, her mouth as kissable as any he'd ever seen, her eyes expressive and gorgeous—at least until she smashed a pair of black-rimmed glasses on her nose.

She wasn't Jon's type of woman, for damn sure. There was no shine, no dazzle, no trimmings on the surface. She clearly wasn't remotely embarrassed about her cluttered place, nor was she running around to fix her hair or smack on lipstick.

She just seemed…real.

Cord wished he could shake off the foggy confusion in his head. He hadn't thought of Zoe in over a year, but now he did—because she was such an elegant example of his poor judgment of women. He'd thought she was the real thing once upon a time, too.

He knew better than to trust anyone too fast—much less to trust his own instincts.

"Cord?" Sophie had clearly been trying to snare his attention for a good minute or two.

"I'm sorry. I was thinking about my brother."

"Of course you were." Her eyes softened in sympathy. "I'll quit babbling, just give you the box of mail. And you can tell me what you decide about Caviar, whenever you get around to it. Right now I assume you're going across the hall to Jon's—"

"Yes."

"So bang on the door if you need anything."

Sophie started humming the minute she closed the door. *That had gone well,* she thought.

For a few moments there, Cord had made her feel uneasy. He just seemed to, well, look at her. Really look. As if he were interested. As if he saw something beyond the black-framed glasses and sisterly smiles and ordinary person.

She retrieved her coffee and plunked herself down at the kitchen table, determined to get an hour or two of translating work done. Naturally, Caviar immediately leaped onto the tabletop and sank, purring, on top of the files she was trying to read. She stroked him absently, musing that probably her restlessness around Cord had an entirely different reason.

Cord was a hunk. Naturally, he'd made her blood spin a little. He had that all-guy walk, the biceps, the crooked smile. He was way beyond adorable. He was sharp, smart, dangerous-looking.

As worrisome as that observation should have been, she yawned as she batted Caviar's paw from the computer screen. Her avatar shot up with the familiar adage: "There's no such thing as being too safe."

Her sisters claimed it was her mantra, which was true. It wasn't that she didn't like men. One of the reasons the traveling in her job had started to nag was that she really wanted a chance to find a guy, settle down, have some kids. But she wanted a man like...well, like her dad. Too many men out there today were all about themselves, treating sex with the casualness of an after-dinner brandy.

She grabbed a pen, scooched Caviar another inch off the papers and heard the phone ring. She picked it up.

No one there, just a hangup.

She settled back down for a solid twenty minutes, when the landline rang again. Again she picked it up.

Again, there was no one on the other side.

Abruptly she stood up, rubbed her hands down her thighs. Not that she spooked easily...but she spooked easily. She had from the time of her parents' death, but her next-door neighbor's death had certainly brought her nerves out of storage. No matter how certain the police were that Jon's death was an accident, Sophie still felt something more had happened.

As if to punctuate her edginess, she jumped when she heard the sudden rap on her front door.

Cord stood on the other side. "I'm sorry to bother you, but..." Caviar shot between her legs, through his and into the open door of Jon's apartment. Cord stared after the loose feline, then back at her, frowning at her expression. "What's wrong? I mean, besides the cat."

"Nothing."

"You're white as a sheet."

"Too much rain. Not enough sun." It was a dumb thing to say, but abruptly she realized her heart had picked up a new, exuberant pounding—not from fear this time. It was from being inches too close to Cord. That problem, thankfully, was readily fixable. "I'll chase after Caviar. The thing is, he's used to being able to shoot back and forth between the two apartments— Oh." Midflight, she stopped abruptly. "I forgot to ask why you knocked on the door. What do you need?"

"Do you know anything about the fancy technology my brother set up in his place?"

"Like what?" She forgot being spooked. The groan in his voice was just funny. Pretty clearly, Cord wasn't the kind of man who tolerated frustration well—or enjoyed asking anyone for help.

She identified the crisis two seconds after entering Jon's apartment.

She'd encountered precisely the same problem the first time she babysat for Caviar. The light switch on the living room east wall didn't turn on lights. It had been rewired to turn on Ravel's "Bolero," close the living room drapes, and start the gas-lit fireplace.

She hiked across the room to the light switch by the drapes, hit it.

The seductive music quit. The gas-lit fire fizzled out. Only the drapes stayed closed.

"What the hell was that?" Cord murmured.

"You don't recognize a staged seduction scene when you see it?"

He scraped a hand through his hair. "Um…to tell you the truth, no."

The thought seeped into her mind that Cord really wouldn't stage anything artificial or contrived with a woman. He wouldn't need to. But she shifted her attention back on track. "You had to know your brother loved gadgets. I always wondered why he didn't make his living as an inventor. Good grief, what's that smell?"

Normally, she'd have waited for an answer before charging into someone else's space, but it was fairly obvious that Cord—no matter how smart—was way, way over his head. No one had been inside the place since the police investigation, and naturally their prime concern hadn't been housekeeping. She had a key, but since Caviar was already safe at her place, she figured she didn't have a reason—or right—to use it.

The bottom line, though, was a symphony of ghastly smells emanating from the kitchen. The sources were easy enough to identify—an uncleaned litter box, some garbage rotting in the disposal and trash, and then there was the opened refrigerator door, which Cord had obviously been trying to clean out.

"That was where I was working," he said. "Obviously, I couldn't do anything else until I cleaned out the rotten fruit and meat, and it was pretty disgusting, so I threw open the window and then walked into the other room for some fresh air. Only, I turned on the living room light—"

"And immediately got stripper music," she said wryly.

He washed a hand over his face. "Look. The smells have to go. And then the place has to be completely aired out before I can pretend to tackle anything else. I don't suppose you'd be up for a walk somewhere? Lunch?"

"I don't think..." But she hesitated. "You want to talk about your brother," she murmured compassionately.

It was his turn to hesitate. "Yeah. Of course I do."

"Okay then. We'll just take a quick break, all right?"

"Right."

* * *

Cord hadn't been lying. He needed fresh air, thinking time away from his brother's place would help to clear out the cobwebs in his head.

More by instinct than intention, he steered Sophie at a brisk pace toward Georgetown. The hike down Pennsylvania Avenue was as peaceful as a tornado drill, between nonstop sirens and barking horns and the occasional thrown-up barrier when a fancy limo or security entourage took over the streets. Oddly, all that craziness struck Cord as comforting. It was just a status quo day around D.C.

What distinctly wasn't status quo was the woman striding next to him.

Looking at the surface facts, Sophie was everything the cops had led him to expect.

She knew his brother's apartment, knew all the details of Jon's corny seduction setup. Very well.

She was jumpy around him, the way a guilty person was jumpy.

And she was so damned easy to be with that he had to believe she could con anyone. God knew, she'd gotten him to readily talk, when Cord had never been a chatterer with anyone.

Of course, he did have stuff he could naturally ask her. "I hate to admit it," he muttered, "but I'm downright confused by my brother's place. I'm not a techno-innocent." An understatement, not that he was going to get into security programs and codes with her. "I can usually get around any computer system. But I don't know what Jon's interest was in all that…gadgetry."

Her chuckle was warmer than sunlight. "I take it you'd never been in your brother's apartment before?"

"No."

"But surely you knew he was a hard-core tinkerer. He seemed to spend his insomnia time inventing stuff that had no use to anyone—except him."

Damn, but she forced him to chuckle now. "Yeah, in a way. I mean, as a kid, no clock or watch was safe around Jon. He loved inventing things, putting spare parts together and coming up with god-knows-what. But I'm finding switches and locks that seem to go nowhere in that apartment."

"Even worse, because he was renting. I'm afraid you'll never get your damage deposit back," she murmured.

By then they'd reached the Potomac. The river was the color of pewter, the skies a matching moody gray. Yet, in spite of the gloom, in spite of the stress surrounding Jon's death, Cord found his spirits lifting from just being around her. Since they'd walked this far, he chose a restaurant he was familiar with—a second-story bar, with a view over the river. She wanted a hot mug of tea; he ordered a tall-necked amber.

"I'm not worried about the damage deposit. I'm just… trying to understand what was going on in his life."

"It doesn't sound as if you and Jon were very close."

"Sure we were. As a close as a cougar and a fox raised in the same den."

"Uh-oh," she murmured, and had him smiling again.

He was honest. No reason not to be. "I keep trying to think back to something Jon and I saw eye to eye on. Maybe we could agree the sky was blue on some summer days, but that's about the end of it."

She cocked her head, her gaze compassionate. "So

you really must feel stuck, having to deal with all his business and stuff."

"I do. But there's no one else to do it, so that's that." He took a long pull from the bottle. "Are you from a big family?"

"Yes and no. Originally there were five of us—my mom and dad, and three girls. I was the baby." She dropped her eyes from his. "Unfortunately, there was a fire when I was around five. We not only lost our parents in one fell swoop, but for a long time we lost each other. No one could foster the three of us together, so we were separated."

"That's not just rough. That's god-awful," he said quietly.

"I have to say…it was. But I was fostered out to a really terrific couple—older—both professors at Georgetown. It was a quiet, safe home in every way. Couldn't have been a more calming situation for a terrorized little kid. They were wonderful to me."

"Are they still around?"

"I only wish. But cancer took Mary a few years ago, and William had a stroke the next year. They were both past sixty when they took me. Anyway, my oldest sister—Cate—never stopped looking for the two of us. She found me first, then Lily. We may not all live in the same city, but we're close enough, phone talk or e-mail talk all the time." She lifted her eyes, "Which is partly why I'm sorry you weren't close with your brother. Family's everything when the road gets rough. As a little girl, I used to have nightmares about being abandoned, lost without anyone. Finding my sisters again has been so great…."

Cord fell silent, trying to imagine a sedate, older

couple taking in a rambunctious five-year-old...and what that must have been like for Sophie, to not only lose her parents, but then her sisters. Yet again, he couldn't fathom that anyone with that background could turn into a money-grubbing, ruthless woman who'd pair with his brother. No matter how he turned those cards around, they just didn't play. If she was a hussy who blackmailed people for sport, he'd eat snails.

More complicated yet, the more he spent time with her, the more he felt an electric, emphatic pull toward her. He wanted to hear more. To look more. To touch.

His grip tightened around the long-necked bottle of beer. "Sophie, you were around Jon enough. Can you tell me what his job was, how he made a living?"

"His job—no. I mean, he used to laugh and say he was a bureaucrat, then just drop it. It's not as if I was in Jon's confidence. The only reason I knew some things was because...well, because he was gone so much. He needed someone around for Caviar, to be there to pick up packages, his mail, that kind of thing. It wasn't one-sided. Whenever I'd leave for the weekend to see my sisters or something like that, he offered to watch over my place the same way."

Cord figured he was going to have to get blunter, or they'd never get down to any brass tacks. "The picture I've gotten...Jon had a lot of women friends."

Color climbed her cheeks. "Yes. I'd say more than 'a lot.'"

"Yet you were always the one he asked to watch the place when he was gone?"

She nodded. "I guess that does seem weird, doesn't it? But actually, he really didn't have women at the apartment all that often. Or if he did, they didn't tend to stay the night." She suddenly tensed up. "Not that I was watching his every move—"

"I didn't mean to suggest you were. I'm just trying to understand anything I can, about his life, about what happened to him. Anything you could tell me would help."

She relaxed again. "Well, as odd as this sounds…I don't think your brother particularly trusted the women he got involved with. I mean, he never seemed to turn down a party. Always seemed to have a good time. But almost no one came back to the apartment more than once. He was kind of like Caviar. Go out and howl in the night, but come back to nest someplace alone when he was tired."

"But he trusted you," Cord pressed.

"I believe he did…but I think for obvious reasons. He looked at me and just didn't see anyone particularly… interesting. Not for him. So we made good neighbors. Seriously good neighbors, actually."

Cord stared at her. She didn't see herself as interesting or sexually appealing to Jon? Or interesting to a man in general, her tone had implied. With that skin, those eyes, that soft red mouth?

For Pete's sake, was she a fabulous fake or the real thing? An award-winning actress or just what she seemed like—the genuine article?

A complex, interesting, and damn beautiful woman.

He spun that word *beautiful* in his mind for a moment. God knew, it wasn't his first impression of her. At first sight, he'd summed her up as frumpy. Lumpy. Dorky.

"What?" she asked warily, when she realized he was staring at her.

"You took off your glasses," he said.

"Oh. I just forget sometimes." Immediately, she popped them back on her nose.

But now he peered closer. They sure as hell looked like clear lenses to him. A disguise. To hide those damn incredible eyes.

Cord resisted the urge to pull out his hair. Whether or not he could trust Sophie should have been clear by now. In the ultraquiet work he'd done for the government, no one had ever doubted his judgment. But then came Zoe, of course. Life-and-death decisions seemed a whole lot easier than any conclusions he could draw about women.

And in the meantime, she'd finished her tea; he'd sure as hell finished his beer, and he had no more answers now than when he'd taken this break.

When he reached for the bill, Sophie leaped to her feet as fast as he did. "I need to get back, too," she said swiftly.

"I never meant to steal this much of your Sunday afternoon."

"I offered to help," she reminded him.

"I know you did. And to tell the truth..." He hesitated. "When we get back, could I ask for a couple more minutes of your time? Not a ton. I'd just appreciate your running through the place, see if you're familiar with any more of my brother's fancy gadgets. I'd just as soon not set off any unintentional alarms."

She smiled. "Sure. In fact...if no one showed you Jon's security setup already, I can do that, too."

A frisky breeze nipped at their cheeks on the walk back. Sophie kept up with his brisk stride, as if she liked a fast pace as much as he did, but Cord noted that she stayed a few inches apart, her hands tucked in her pockets, as if making a point not to encourage any physical contact. Still, she kept shooting him quiet glances.

Both of them were probably doing the same thing. Cord suspected she had her own reasons for sizing him up, measuring who he was—especially because she obviously didn't have too high an opinion of his brother.

Once back at the Foggy Bottom brownstone, she came in, as asked, but she made a point of not shedding her jacket—just started a free-flow information spill. It wasn't babbling. She really knew a lot about Jon's apartment.

"The thing is, Cord, a hundred years ago, this building was a single-family residence—so my half of the upstairs isn't a mimic of your brother's. Jon's side is bigger. But it's more than that. The odd shape of Jon's kitchen is probably because it was once a bedroom...."

He'd been through the place before, obviously, but Sophie made him see the layout with new eyes. Jon may have picked an old place because architecturally, there were more ways to hide things. The kitchen may have once been a bedroom, but it was predictably stuffed with new appliances and gadgets. The red-and-black bathroom had been outfitted with a towel warmer, a disappearing steam machine, a cupboard that revealed a chilled square—for drinks? Food? God knew.

Still, past the living room and kitchen and bedroom was the only beyond-weird room in the flat. Cord stood in the doorway, hands on hips, feeling as if he'd just stepped into a sci-fi setting. Sophie ambled right in. "I never saw Jon's bedroom, so I don't know what's in there. But this was your brother's...sandbox, so to speak. The room where he played. And it's the room he told me most about, because when he was gone for a night or two, he worried about the security in here."

Cord knew computers and security setups, but nothing remotely like this. Not for a private citizen, anyway. A square platform desk took up the room's center, covered with four functioning computers and symbiotic hardware. Writhing snakes of electric cords tangled every which way. Beneath the single window was a long bench table, obviously a worktable of some kind.

"No," Sophie said suddenly.

"What?"

"You don't want to touch that picture," she warned him.

"Why?" For some insane reason, Jon had hung an incongruous and tasteless picture of a naked Mona Lisa on the inside wall. Sophie suddenly showed up beside him, touched "the smile"—and all the computers abruptly when blank.

She touched the eyes in the painting, and throughout the room, locks turned on all the desk and file drawers.

And then she chuckled at Cord's expression. "I know. I can't imagine why Jon did it, either. He just seemed to have fun with this kind of thing. He was always afraid I'd come in to feed Caviar when he was gone and I'd touch something by mistake."

She motioned to a specific tile in the checkerboard floor. "If you step on that square, you'll set off an alarm in the kitchen. Caviar's done it a few times, although I think Cav's figured out most of Jon's booby traps by now. You see that weird little square quilt on the wall? It really is a quilt, but if you poke it, it opens up to a mini bar, with drinks and glasses. It shares the same wall as the kitchen, and he put this in so he didn't have to walk all the way around the hall to get a drink and put in his dirty dishes. Jon was on the lazy side. And then..."

She shifted past him, leading him back toward the kitchen. "I know you've already seen this room, but this drawer here—" She pulled at the latch, revealing the usual catchall utensil drawer everybody had, the one that held a hammer and screwdriver and flashlight and all the junk that refused to belong anywhere else. "The drawer doesn't have a false bottom, but see? There's a row of three buttons here. The first shoots the dead bolts on the front and back doors. The middle one shuts off all the lights in the house. Pretty silly, if you ask me. Why would you want to be standing in the kitchen in a dark house? Anyway. The third one...um, shoot. Your brother only told me about this stuff once, and I never thought about it again. I forgot what Jon told me the third button was for."

She glanced up with an impish smile, clearly wanting to share humor at his brother's idiosyncratic ideas.

Cord was inches away from her at that second. Inches away from that smile, those silly glasses. Inches away from the woman who'd been confounding him from the minute he met her. From the very beginning, he was uncertain whether she was saint or sinner...angel or thief...a truly fascinating woman or a manipulative sociopath.

But it was about time he found out.

So maybe a kiss wasn't alchemy. Maybe there was no miracle test to definitively separate the truth from the lies. But he knew *something* definitive the instant his mouth dropped on hers.

He lifted his head with a frown. She lifted her head with the same perplexed frown.

Some instinct made him pluck the glasses from her nose, set them on the counter, then go back for another kiss. This one involved tongues and teeth and pressure. This one involved framing her head in his hands and closing his eyes.

Her mouth was softer than butter. The way she stilled reminded him of a doe in a buck's sights. She went soft-still, worried—still…yet she didn't bolt. Cautiously, carefully, her lips returned the pressure, as if she were sampling him no differently than he, as he was getting a serious, deep taste of her.

And then her arms reached out, reached up, the bulk of her jacket making a whiskery sound when her hands locked behind his neck. A groan, helpless and vulnerable, shuddered from the very back of her throat. Suddenly she was up on tiptoe, kissing him back, offering her mouth, her tongue. She was like…a firecracker. It was as if a fuse suddenly lit, a spark that suddenly flared into a female combustible firestorm in three seconds flat.

Or maybe that was ten seconds.

And maybe six or seven kisses had passed by then, because he seemed to have hooked his arms around her waist and lifted her up to the counter. She was too damn short to bend down to kiss—at least to kiss the right way—for very long.

He told himself he had outstanding reasons to be suspicious. She was trouble. To the bone.

And God knew, he had a hard one by then.

Only, she kissed with the wild winsomeness of an untried virgin. Expressing yearning. Need. And hunger—the shaking-out-of-control kind, the vulnerable kind, the kind you never unlocked your doors for unless you were damned sure what kind of partner you were dealing with.

Finally he tore his mouth free from hers. Needing oxygen. Needing sanity. Frowning at her with even deeper, darker frustration than when they'd first started this. "What the hell was that?" he muttered.

She was breathing hard, too, her face flushed and her mouth wet—and she glowered at him with the same impatience. "Don't you mess with me, Cord."

*"Me?"*

"I'm not a player. If you're like your brother, just move on. There are many super women out there. Lots of women looking for fun. Or just a good game. That's not me. Leave me alone if that's what you're looking for."

"I wasn't looking for anything."

"Well, I wasn't, either," she said grumpily, and slid off the counter. She moved past him, called out, "Caviar!"

The mangy thing appeared instantly, shot Cord a look and an annoyed flick of his tail, then took off with Sophie. He heard the door slam. Then they were both gone.

*Okay,* he thought. *Okay...that had really proved something.*

What, he had no idea.

Except that he needed to sit down before he fell down. For days, there'd been nothing on his mind but his brother's killer. Now, all he could think about was a far more enticing danger.

*Damn, but that woman could kiss.*

# Chapter 4

Sophie switched off her recorder and stood up. "You've been wonderful, Mrs. Hoffman." It had been a productive Monday afternoon, but she could see her eighty-one-year-old interviewee was wilted now.

"You've brought my memories to life again, child," Mrs. Hoffman answered in German. She, too, stood up, with the help of a cane. "No one ever listened to my side before."

"They should have." Maybe it was a job, but Sophie still leaned over to kiss Mrs. Hoffman's cheek. Before gathering up her work and jacket, she carted the German porcelain cup to the miniature kitchen in the back. Mrs. Hoffman always served some kind of fancy tea, but Sophie didn't want the elderly woman cleaning up after her.

Her mind was still spinning from the stories Greta

Hoffman had shared. She'd been just a girl when Hitler had invaded "her" Austria. She remembered a boisterously noisy city turning suddenly silent.

"People who talked suddenly disappeared—or were just plain shot down on the street, as if they were rabid dogs," Mrs. Hoffman recounted. "Men used to go to the beer gardens to talk politics—that stopped. Women used to chatter with neighbors at the grocer's—that all stopped. After the war, when people kept saying, how could you have let this happen, how could you not have known? About the gas chambers. The Jews."

Sophie had heard this before, all through these hours of interviews, but Greta's eyes were lonely and sad, lost in her old memories.

"What people didn't understand is that we were all afraid. To speak against Hitler meant death. Day by day, month by month, more and more people disappeared. We knew they were dead. In our hearts, we knew. But we were all frightened of dying, too. So we walked with our heads down and we hid in our houses. My father…I still remembered his slapping my face. I'd laughed at something. On the street. Laughed out loud, drawing attention to myself. My father had never hit me before…."

It was another half hour before Sophie could make it to the door and really mean her "goodbye" this time.

"It was the whispers that were dangerous," Mrs. Hoffman echoed again. "Any whisper of a transgression could bring on certain death. You didn't have to do anything wrong. You were judged by those rumors alone. You think whispers have no power…but they do, child, they do."

Night had fallen hard and cold by the time Sophie

climbed onto the metro. From there she walked the few blocks home, carrying the usual ten tons of equipment and satchels, on crackling leaves, through wisps of fog.

She'd thought of Cord all day—and all last night—yet now Mrs. Hoffman's words made her think of him in a different context. Greta's comments about whispers and rumors nailed the whole atmosphere around D.C. Some said the city thrived on the power of whispers.

Cord's brother had sure seemed to thrive on whispers and intrigue.

Sophie crossed the road, heard a horn blare at her lack of attention, and then hustled the last half block toward home. She wished she knew whether Cord thrived on intrigue the way his brother had.

The kisses from the day before had haunted her sleep, her daydreams...like a whisper that only her heart could hear. There was no shutting it off.

She wasn't dead positive she wanted those heart whispers to shut down. She'd liked those kisses.

She liked Cord. He was sharp, easy to talk to, interesting to be with. He provoked a razzle-dazzle in her hormones that she hadn't felt in a long time. Yearning. Heat. All that good wickedness.

Somewhere in the apartment, she had an old photo from when she was a little girl, wearing a pink scarf of her mom's like a boa, holding a hairbrush for a fake microphone, dramatically pelting out a song at the top of her lungs. Apparently, as a kid, she'd been quite a rowdy, show-off ham. An extrovert to the nth degree. A singer, a dancer, a weaver of daisies.

But her foster parents had needed a quiet, well-behaved child, a good girl. So she'd become one. When you lost everyone and everything that ever mattered to you, you didn't need to sing. You needed to survive.

Caution had become a religion for her. She'd positively never risked much with men. Yet, she'd wanted to yesterday afternoon. For a few moments, caution had disappeared and that wild, rowdy girl-child had whispered through her heart again with Cord.

*Stop it, Soph.* She pushed open the door, dug out her mailbox key, aggravated that she was daydreaming again. Some wary instinct warned her that Cord was holding back something serious. Actually, it would have been weird if he didn't. They barely knew each other, no reason he should have shared private things with her. And his brother's death was complicated.

The point, though, was that she needed to rein herself in until she knew more about him.

Not that he was likely to invite her for any more kisses, anyway.

As she tromped up the stairs, she decided she needed to get her mind off Cord altogether. A plan came together—she'd kick back, pop a glass of wine, settle with Caviar on the couch and call her sisters. She had her apartment key out, because sometimes even a scatterbrain such as herself could have a bright moment…only to abruptly discover that she wouldn't need it.

Her apartment door gaped open.

She could hear the cat meowing from a distance inside.

Confused, she took a single step in…and felt her heart start slamming like a manic drum. Her living room was in shambles. Books and knickknacks had been tumbled off shelves. A broken lamp strewed shards on the carpet.

Couch cushions looked as if they'd been ripped apart by shark's teeth.

She sucked in a breath, and let it out in one loud screech for Caviar.

When the authorities arrived this time, she was sitting on the top step in the hall, still wearing her coat, the scrawny cat cuddled on her lap. She considered it a miracle she'd been able to punch in 911. Her fingers were still shaking. *She* was still shaking.

One trauma in a week was enough. As far as Sophie was concerned, two traumas were grounds for major hysteria. If she wanted to fold in a puddle and blubber for a good long time, she was entitled.

Two policemen showed up this time. The first, she remembered from before, because, humorously, he looked a little like a bleary-eyed bloodhound. Ed or George. Bassett, she thought. He took one look at her and sighed.

She'd sensed he hadn't liked her when they first met, and this time he looked even more annoyed. "You're developing an interesting pattern of attracting trouble, Ms. Campbell. Bad trouble. Now, why is that?"

Her jaw almost dropped. It was as if he were accusing her of causing this. "Detective, I just got home from work and found the door open. I haven't a clue who would do this. Or why."

"If you thought a burglar was inside your place, I find it interesting that you didn't run like hell instead of staying right here."

Again, Sophie couldn't grasp what he was getting at. "I couldn't just take off. There was Caviar."

"Yeah. Right." He let out another noisy, exasperated

sigh, accompanied by another judgmental look. Eventually, his younger sidekick—a kid with fuzz on his chin and shiny shoes—hunched down beside her with paper and pen to take her statement, while Detective Meanie Bassett disappeared inside to examine the crime scene. She asked if she could get a glass of water, but the kid insisted that she wait, that she wasn't supposed to enter her apartment until the detective gave an all clear.

Apparently, she could contaminate things. God forbid her fingerprints could show up in her own apartment. The hall was chilly and gloomy. She was tired and stressed when a third man showed up.

He shook her hand, identified himself as Ian Ferrell. He was older than Bassett, leaner than wire, sharp faced and sharp eyed. Sophie had no idea why she sensed this Ferrell was more in charge than the detective, but the minute he got there, things changed.

He wanted her to go into the apartment—with him. It was totally okay if she took a drink and took a minute in the bathroom, but then he wanted to walk through every room slowly with her. He wanted her to identify anything that was missing, also anything that had been moved or looked out of place. "Just study everything. Look past the damage. See if you can pinpoint specifically what the suspect was after."

"You're giving me the impression that you don't believe this was a run-of-the-mill robbery," she said anxiously.

"It could be. But we want to examine all the possibilities." Ferrell seemed to be studying her more than the scene, particularly when she shuddered hard at the close-up of her living room.

Nothing she owned was particularly valuable, but

everything had been handpicked and loved. She had nothing from her childhood but a few worn photos, certainly no belongings or keepsakes. It was as if the Campbell family had never existed. Sophie couldn't imagine a reason in the universe why anyone would have ripped up the rental sofa, or yanked the books from the shelves, or opened up a lamp-table drawer that had nothing but scissors and thread and nail files and hand cream. What possible reason could anyone have to do this?

Yet, the way Ferrell kept studying her made something click in her mind. "You don't think this is a chance robbery, do you?" More clicks followed that first one. "Two crimes in the same building within a week is just too much coincidence? But, Mr. Ferrell, Jon's death was ruled an accident. Why would you think there was a relationship?"

"No one said there was," Ferrell said patiently.

Sophie decided she must be crazy or something. The authorities seemed to be treating her as if she were guilty, instead of the victim—how paranoid could a girl get? Obviously, she wasn't thinking straight. And how could she, given the state of her home? The darned thief had upended all eight purses in her closet. Her computer had been turned on. All her CDs and disks taken. At Ferrell's urging, she checked her hard drive, which seemed to have all her data files intact, but it would take her hours of messing with it to be certain.

Bassett intervened at that point, told her they wanted to take her system with them.

"What? You can't do that. I need it. It's got all my work on it—" Well, that wasn't totally true, because she had her laptop. Her laptop was her secondary backup.

But that wasn't the point. The point was that this whole mess was spinning out of control. She had two solid days of translating work to do on her system. The police heard her; they just didn't seem to care. Being broken into felt like…an assault. Someone who'd never lost their home and family might not get how huge a violation this was. A stranger had touched the things of her heart. Broken them, diminished them. And on top of her neighbor's traumatic death last week, it was just too much.

"Taking the desktop is necessary," Bassett said, as if that should settle it.

Nothing was settled, as far as Sophie was concerned. The search continued. Her hands got shakier and her stomach queasier. The thief had pilfered through her freezer. What on *earth* had he expected to find there? And in her bedroom, drawers were yanked open, her lingerie and jewelry strewn all over the place, her mom's pearls abandoned on the floor. The state of the pearls made her eyes sting more than anything else. She ran to pick them up—or tried to.

"No, Ms. Campbell," Ian Ferrell said gently, "The best chance for us to find prints is to work with the items we know the perpetrator touched."

Sophie hadn't had a temper tantrum since she was five. She never lost it. Ever. But tarnation, she was coming darn close. "Those are my mother's pearls. *No one* is taking my mother's pearls or touching my mother's pearls. That's it, guys. That's the line. I mean it—"

"Listen, Ms. Campbell," Ferrell said patiently, "our guys will probably be here for just a couple of hours. Do you have somewhere you could go? There isn't anything else you can help us with, so you could get some fresh air."

"I don't want fresh air, and I'm not leaving the cat."

"Now just think," Bassett said flatly, "you're not going to feel safe staying here alone tonight anyway, are you? I'm sure the cat will be fine. And tomorrow morning, if you wouldn't mind coming down to the station to make a statement—"

"Are you guys crazy or am I? I've already made a statement. I've told you everything I know. I'm the one who's the victim here, remember?"

At the precise moment she was about to wring George Bassett's jowly neck—or let a bunch of frustrated tears spring loose—she saw Cord striding in her front door.

Maybe she wasn't the kind of woman to depend on a hero—and she hadn't lived a life where she could possibly need one—but when he met her eyes, she flew toward him faster than a thief for a bank vault. He had her tucked under his shoulder in two seconds flat.

Every sensory nerve in her body took him in. His face was windburned, his pulse fast, as if he'd been running. He was wearing old corduroys and his battered sheepskin jacket, and he hadn't shaved. The feel of his scratchy chin on her forehead, the heat and strength of his long, tall body—she couldn't remember such a sense of belonging with someone else. Maybe she was just traumatized, but who cared? Damn but he felt good.

"You needed more hell, did you?" he murmured.

Naturally, she was curious how he'd showed up right then, but she didn't ask. She didn't care. "This has been a nightmare," she said helplessly. "I can't imagine why anyone would have done this to me. Why, how, who—

anything. So much wealth around here, why would anyone pick on me?"

He didn't answer, just took charge—not in a big, noisy way. He just stepped in, intervened. The next few minutes passed in such a blur that they barely registered. She noticed something in the way Bassett and Ferrell responded to his showing up, the way they talked to him—they knew Cord.

If that should have alerted something on her internal wary scale, it didn't. Nothing did.

"I'm taking her out of here for a while," Cord told the cops. "Get her something to eat, a drink."

She said, "Caviar's traumatized. I really don't want to leave him alone."

Cord noted the cat cuddled under her coat, gently hooked the mangy feline under an arm and escorted him to her bed in the other room. "He's a tomcat," he reminded her. "I do believe he's had a few terrorizing experiences in the past and survived them."

"But he's a tomcat who came in from the cold. He wants shelter now. I don't want to let him down."

"Sophie."

"What?"

"You're not letting him down," he said patiently. "We're just getting out of here for a few minutes. Grab some food. Find a quiet place to just chill for a while. Then we'll come back here. I'll sleep next door. You won't be alone. The cat won't be alone. How's that for a plan?"

It was a good plan. It was the best plan she'd ever heard. She wanted to be with Cord and away from here, more than anything she could imagine wanting.

But the complete trust she wanted to feel with him

wasn't quite there. She wanted it to be. Sophie knew perfectly well she was a sissy in the guy department, too damned afraid of being abandoned to give trust unless she had every lock latched, every T crossed, every possible question out on the table. But still…she couldn't just make those worry buzzers in her heart totally shut off.

"I should call my sisters. And Jan and Hillary and Penelope—the neighborhood women. They'll have seen the cop cars. They'll be concerned."

"So bring your cell," Cord said.

*Well, sheesh.* After that, she couldn't think of any more objections.

Bassett and Ferrell undoubtedly thought he was going along with their plans by getting Sophie out of the way, but Cord's motivation came from an entirely different source.

Outside, his car was double-parked—not an uncommon occurrence around D.C.—but at the cost of tickets, a lot easier to pull off when you had the authorities' permission. Sophie didn't seem to notice where he was parked. When he helped her into the passenger seat of his Bronc, she flinched at the passing lights of a cop car. By the time he'd started the engine, his jaw felt glued together.

She looked more fragile than a rose petal. Fragile, crushable and damned scared. She got out her cell phone, obviously intending to call her sisters and friends, but for a few moments she just sat silently, locked in her seat belt and folded up inside her jacket as if hoping she could disappear.

Cord weaved in and out of traffic, turning right on

Pennsylvania, his veins pumping adrenaline. He wished she could do exactly that—disappear. The woman was in danger. And because the cops thought Sophie was guilty of something, they weren't going to protect her. They wanted to use her.

It was Ferrell who'd called him, and that message was still ringing in his mind. Ferrell told him about the break-in, told him if there was ever a good shot at getting information out of Sophie Campbell, it was now. She could have staged the break-in herself, to divert suspicion. If she hadn't, then whoever Cord's brother had been blackmailing believed that Sophie either had the evidence—or knew where it was.

Jon's autopsy had come back. There'd been two critical blows—one to the back of the head, one to the forehead. The latter had propelled him down the stairs, and was how he'd ended up lying on his back, but it had been the first blow that had really been the killer. There was no hard evidence to pin down the culprit, but according to Bassett, it was either a woman or a short man.

The cops had figured the killer as a woman from the start. More than ever, they wanted Cord to grill Sophie. Or as Ferrell put it, grill her or seduce her. Whatever worked to get information from her.

Cord's grip tightened on the wheel while he listened to her calling friends on her cell phone. She left messages for her sisters, didn't reach Hillary, but connected to Jan Howell…who questioned her on every detail, what happened, what the cops said, what she'd said, making promises to tell everyone else so she didn't have to repeat the call, offering to immediately come over—on and on.

When Sophie hung up, she leaned back against the seat as if too wiped out to hold her head up.

"Hillary…she's the one with the extraordinary, um…?" Cord had a hard time keeping the brunettes straight.

"Boobs. Yes." Sophie didn't open her eyes. "That figure of hers is so ironic. She's soft-spoken, very shy, and a doctor—smarter than any ten people I know. Yet all people notice are her looks."

"Hard not to."

"I know. Women prejudge her, too. I'm just saying… she's a true-blue kind of person."

In Sophie's judgment, Cord mused. "And Jan, the friend you did manage to reach. She's the real tall glass of water, looks like she dresses at an art museum? The one who starts shooting the bull before she's even said hello?"

Sophie opened one eye then. "She was great to me when I first moved here and knew nobody."

Which meant, Cord figured, that she didn't think a whole lot of Jan, either, but wasn't about to knock someone who'd been good to her. "She was a friend of my brother's?"

"Cord, every woman in the neighborhood knew your brother, and more than ninety percent, I'd guess, made a play for him. I never kept track of who he slept with. I didn't care. Still don't."

She changed subjects. "I don't want to be gone for too long."

"We'll be back in a couple hours, no more. Are you hungry for anything special?"

"I couldn't possibly eat a thing," she assured him.

Uh-huh. He used his cell to order takeout. In less

than an hour, he'd picked up the brown bag, spread out a stadium blanket from the trunk and had Sophie installed on the grass with a view of the Washington Monument. She plowed through the War Sui Gui, then the Shrimp Fried Rice, then two egg rolls and a little Steak Kow.

Cord started to worry if he'd bought enough. The blanket wasn't much protection against the cold ground, but her jacket was warm enough for the Arctic, and overall, she just seemed to calm down. "I love the Washington Monument," she said—or tried to say. Her mouth was pretty full.

"Yeah, me, too. Hate politics. Hate a lot about Washington. But when I look at the monument lit up at night…"

"It gives me shivers. Good shivers."

It didn't give him shivers, but something was right about this place, this time, this country. Her. Him. Although, once she'd inhaled all that food, she lost some of that lost look and started talking.

"Both those policemen knew you," she said in an accusing tone.

"Yeah, of course they did."

"Why 'of course'?"

"Because they're the ones who told me about Jon's death. I've spent more hours with them than I'd care to count." When she tucked up her legs and didn't respond further, he pushed with a "What?"

"There's something you're not telling me. Something everybody's not telling me. Something's…wrong."

"Of course there is. Two serious crimes took place in your apartment building in less than two weeks."

"That part, I get. What I don't understand is why I keep getting the feeling the police are hiding information from me. As if they know something about who might have vandalized my place, but for some reason they don't want to tell me the whole story."

There were others out, enjoying the night. People always loved seeing the monuments at night, and lovers traditionally used the strolls around the mall to snuggle together. Yards away, Cord heard the hum of conversation, a woman's whispers.

The only whispers he wanted to hear, though, were Sophie's. Her hair looked like a spill of silver in the starlight, her eyes liquid dark. Magical. He wasn't the kind to believe in magic or spells…yet, there was something he couldn't explain when he was with Sophie. For one thing, he knew perfectly well the cops didn't want him telling her the truth.

Yet, how could he possibly protect her if she didn't understand more of the bigger picture?

"Sophie…I think the police don't totally trust you."

Her response was an immediate chuckle. "Of course they do. Everyone trusts me!" She pointed to her face, as if it would be obvious to anyone looking at her that she couldn't fib without broadcasting it to the universe.

But when he looked at her face, all he could think of was wanting to kiss it. To see her eyes widen with vulnerability. To see those soft red lips part, to let him in. Just him. Only him.

Hell. Where had that come from?

He tried to get back on track. "The police think you might have some idea what the thief wanted from your apartment."

"How am I possibly supposed to know what that could be?"

He said patiently, "From what Bassett said…you had

a stash of money in your cookie jar. A hundred bucks. No one took it. You had some jewelry, but no one took that, either. Computer, TV, electronics—all the stuff thieves go for was still there. So the thief had to want something else. And maybe that 'something' is related to my brother's death—because why else would the two traumatic incidents take place in the same building, within two weeks of each other?"

She cocked her head, looked at him with such empathy. "Cord, I understand why you want there to be a reason for your brother's death. The fire that killed my parents…it haunted my sisters and me for years. We just wanted there to be a reason, some way to make sense of what happened, something we could blame. But there was never a reason, not that anyone could find. I know it's hard. I know. Even if you weren't close to your brother, I totally understand why you feel pushed to find a reason for his death, something that mattered. Something that could help you put closure on the loss…"

Guilt felt like a coffin nail. He hated not being able to totally fill her in. Sophie still didn't know Jon's death was a murder. The authorities had honest reasons for keeping the cause of death quiet, but that failed to appease his conscience. Her warm compassion bit. He knew he hadn't earned her sympathy.

"Sophie…" He'd brought a bottle of wine with the take-out dinner. Maybe wine wasn't precisely legal out there in the open, but she stopped looking so white and anxious after a couple of paper cups. He poured her a little more. "We're not talking about me. We're talking about you. About any reasons you can imagine why someone might have broken into your place. Think."

She took another sip. "Well…my foster parents left me a nest egg. At the time they took me in, they were considered too old to adopt, by the rules then. But they created a trust for me, because they knew…" She gulped again. "They knew I had nightmares for years, about losing my home, my parents, my family, everything. They didn't want me to be afraid that could ever happen again. So they wanted me to have something to fall back on. But, Cord, I can't imagine anyone knows about that but my sisters. I've traveled too much with my job to have accumulated much, and I'm pretty sure no one would say I run around looking wealthy."

He definitely wouldn't say that. She ran around in clothes and colors that made her look nondescript—and he was beginning to understand why. She didn't want trouble. She did everything but stand on her head to not attract trouble, any kind of trouble…so this whole mess had to be her worst nightmare.

Her revealing the business about her nest egg showed that she trusted him—was risking her trust on him.

That alone revealed her innocence to him, in both senses of the word. The more he knew her, the more time he spent with her, the more beautiful he could see she was. The wrong kind of beauty. The dangerous kind of beauty. The true-blue vulnerability in her eyes was the kind that could attract the worst predators. And Cord sure as hell couldn't be the only man who saw beneath the silly clothes and glasses to the Sophie underneath.

Impatiently, he said, "Come on, Soph. There has to be something else."

This conversation was getting nowhere—at least not in the direction it was supposed to go. The more Cord believed in Sophie's innocence, the more he realized that the guilty party, the one who murdered his brother, was still out there free. And Sophie was a stop sign in the way.

Sophie shrugged her shoulders. "You keep saying there has to be something else. But I've told you all the something elses I can think of, Cord."

He tugged at the collar of her jacket when he caught her shivering. "When the police looked into Jon's death, they were uneasy about some loose ends. They had the impression Jon was hiding something."

"You mean drugs?"

"Not drugs. But something that explains all the trap doors and hidey-holes and locked gadgets in his apartment. I don't have the whole picture," he said, with complete honesty. "But I'm getting enough to be… worried. And now someone's ransacked your place."

She shook her head in bewilderment. "You're making it sound as if you believe there's a connection."

Cord had had it with juggling what he could tell her and what he couldn't. Maybe he couldn't tell her the authorities' "truth." But he could sure as hell choose to share his own. "I believe my brother was involved in something unsavory. Even as a kid, he was always looking for ways to make a buck without having to do anything as annoying as real work. The way this appears, I think Jon had information about certain important people. Affairs, mistakes—that kind of thing. I don't know who or what. But I believe his 'victims' want that information back, and are particularly worried what happened to it since Jon died."

Sophie gulped down more wine and held out her paper cup. "No matter what the police said, you don't think your brother's death was an accident, do you?"

"Nope. I don't."

She waggled her cup. "More wine."

"Don't you think you've had quite a bit?"

"Not if we're going to talk about murder."

He filled her cup again and quit arguing.

# *Chapter 5*

Amazing what a little wine and food could do. Granted, she was seeing streetlights in triplicate and her head felt a little woozy…but she wasn't scared anymore.

She was mad.

"I never get mad," she told Cord.

"So you've mentioned, several times."

"It's an amazing relief. Instead of feeling scared, to just let go and feel *mad*. I mean, what is this?" She waved her arms to illustrate. "I've had enough rotten stuff to deal with. Getting broken into is just ridiculously unfair. Finding your dead brother was even worse. I mean, maybe your brother wasn't the most ethical knife in the drawer, but…" She frowned, not certain if she was making sense. Although that didn't seem to stop her from talking. "I'm going to get regularly mad from now on. Loud mad. *Mean mad.* It's so much better than being scared. When I was a little girl, I used to stand on the porch and sing at the top of my lungs, did you know that? I was a brat. A ham. An attention grabber. It took years, *years,* to turn me into the pissy, button-down fuddy-duddy I am today… Oh God, did I say pissy? I meant prissy. I would never say prissy…I mean pissy… oh, shoot, which one *did* I mean?"

"Sophie, let's wait until the car stops before you get out, cookie."

"And then there's you," she muttered. Fresh air slapped her in the face when she climbed out of the car. Good thing, since the whole street was revolving like a carousel. Suddenly, she wondered why she didn't drink more often. This was so wonderful. The whole night looked magically sprinkled with stardust.

"Sophie?"

"No," she said firmly, and abruptly danced down the street. Cord did that to her. Made her feel like dancing. Made her think about moonlight and stardust. It was… unsettling. Somewhere beneath the taste of all that wine was the taste of temptation. Not the temptation of stardust, but the temptation of plain old lust. No man had tempted her in years—not *really* tempted—the kind of temptation that made her want to strip off more than clothes. The kind of temptation to throw all her fears to the wind and just grab hold of him for the lust of it.

"Oh, no," she muttered. "I learned a long time ago that monsters don't hide under the bed. They're everywhere. At least *my* monsters are. You can't feel safe if you think someone's going to disappear on you. And they all do. Everyone does. So, for darn sure, you don't open the door to someone you're not sure of. And for damn sure, I'm not sure of you."

Abruptly, she found Cord standing directly in front of her. "I haven't a clue what you're talking about, Soph, but your apartment is that way." He motioned behind her.

"Well, hell. Who moved my building?" she demanded.

If he answered her, she couldn't hear him—possibly because her right ear was abruptly crushed against his chest. His long arm tucked her against his side as he turned her around, steering her toward the brownstone. She'd have protested, but the truth was that she'd have stumbled if he hadn't helped hold her up.

Still, she felt the situation needed clarifying. "Look," she said, "I don't do this. Ever."

"Don't do what?"

"I don't fall in love with men who aren't honest with me. Cripes, it's hard enough for me to loosen up with men who *are* honest with me. You're too far off my radar, Cord. There's no reason you'd normally be looking at me. So something isn't kosher. I feel it. I *know* it. So that's it. I'm not falling in love with you. It'd be like getting a love note from a pistachio."

"Huh?"

"You don't know the pistachio song? You want me to sing it?"

"No. Please God, no. Sophie, just concentrate on walking, okay?"

"Or I could sing the other song, about walking on the safe side of the sidewalk. About how she's afraid to trust anyone, even herself. That's me. The untruster. The safe sidewalk walker." She repeated that phrase, charmed with herself. All those *S*'s and *W*'s. And she said them brilliantly. Several times.

Out of the complete blue, Cord suddenly lifted her in his arms.

"What—"

"Shh. No more talking for you."

Well, the truth was, she was pretty darned exhausted. So she closed her eyes for just a second, thinking she just needed a moment to catch her breath.

Just before opening her eyes, Sophie felt the snuggly security of a warm, breathing body next to her. A male body. And so typical of a male who'd gotten exactly what he wanted, he was purring loud enough to wake the neighborhood.

"Caviar, you *know* you're not allowed under the covers...." Her groggy voice trailed off abruptly. Caviar didn't seem to be the only male in her bedroom.

Cord looked downright silly, sprawled in her white wicker rocker with the flowery cushion. He'd taken off his shoes. His right sock had a hole. His hair looked raked by a tornado and his chin had sprouted a weed patch of whiskers.

He was also awake. Glaring at her with those sexy dark eyes...although the shadows under his eyes were bigger than boats.

"What on earth are you doing here?" she said groggily.

"You scared the hell out of me."

"I scared *you?*"

"You had a ton of food, you know. A *ton*. I thought the wine would help you calm down. When we first left, I could see how shaken up you were by the break-in. And you only had half the bottle. It was just *wine*. After all that food. I take it you don't normally drink?"

"Is this your way of apologizing for getting me drunk?" She peeked under the covers. Caviar looked up at her with sleepy eyes. Nothing else under there but her in all her clothes—except for her shoes—and the cat.

"I didn't get you drunk. I was trying to be helpful, for God's sake."

She leaned up on an elbow. He'd stayed there all night, just because he was worried about her?

But then the rest of life came back into focus. Daylight filtered through the north window, illuminating part of the devastation from the night before. Her tall, antique-white bookcase with the glass doors—hers, not part of the rental furniture that came with the place—was in shambles, glass panes broken, books spilled all over the polished plank floors. Her shoes and purses looked strewn from her closet by a drunk ogre on a binge. Drawers were askew, revealing bra straps and socks and an upended box of old letters.

"You *were* helpful," she said to Cord. "I don't care if I had too much wine. I needed to get away from this for a little bit. But now..."

Now she had a monster mess—and a job—to attend to, and she assumed he'd leave. Instead, when she got out of the bathroom, fresh showered, still pulling a purple sweater over her pounding head, Cord was still there.

She found him in the kitchen, by following the smell of fresh coffee and the sound of crackling eggs, but he stopped messing with the spatula the instant she walked in. Talk about an inspection. She felt examined, from her gray flannel skirt to the bulky fit of her purple sweater to her fresh-washed hair. His gaze narrowed on her face, though. "You don't feel sick?" he asked her.

"Sick at the mess from the break-in, yes. Sick because of the wine, no. *What?*"

He motioned her to sit at the table—where he'd miraculously cleared a spot for a plate and fork, as if he owned the place. Next to the napkin, though, was a thick manila envelope. "Don't touch it," he said. "I'm taking it to the police this morning. But I wanted you to see it first. It was in my brother's mailbox this morning."

She picked up the china cup of coffee at the same time she glanced at the envelope's contents. And then slapped down the cup abruptly.

"Good grief," she said.

"I didn't count it. I grabbed a paper towel so I wouldn't get my fingerprints on it. But as far as I can tell..."

"These are *hundreds* of hundred-dollar bills. Holy cow. Holy smokes. There must be thousands of dollars in there."

"Yeah." He let out an exasperated sigh. "No note, no nothing to identify the sender. Looks pretty obviously like blackmail money to me. I don't know why else anyone would be sending Jon cash—not cash like this. And whoever the sender was, apparently he—or she—didn't know Jon was dead."

She stared at him in shock.

But Cord wasn't through talking. "Sophie," he said quietly, "I need your help. I know the police will do what they can, but I just don't have total faith in their ability to figure this out—at least fast enough to prevent any more trouble. I have to find out what Jon was up to. I wish it weren't your problem, but damn it, it is. Once they broke into your place, it became your problem, too. You're not safe. I don't know how to make you safe until we've got an answer for this."

* * *

Two days could make an amazing difference. Her apartment was full of noise and laughter. Caviar had strategically located himself on top of the living room bookshelf, where he could regard the group of women with a slit-eyed, appalled expression. Down at coffee-table level, the remnants of a pizza, sodas and paper plates covered that space. The floor was more littered with cleaning supplies and trash bags than the cat could survive.

"You guys are being so wonderful," Sophie said helplessly.

"Oh, shut up, Soph. You'd do the same for us." Jan, looking like a moon goddess in a tie-dyed silver smock dress, had been the first to show up after work. She'd taken on the job of keeping everyone fed and watered—at least when she wasn't nosing around Sophie's bookshelves and drawers and all. "You know, if you'd just give me a budget and some permission, I could turn this place into something else. It's got gorgeous architecture."

"I think the last thing Soph is worried about right now is color schemes." Hillary had popped in after a shift at the hospital. She'd taken off her lab coat, revealing jeans and a white sweater. On her, the outfit looked runway-ready. She'd installed herself in front of Sophie's computer, and was analyzing what damage the vandal had done to the files and records.

"Well, I want to hear about Jon's brother." Penelope, after spending a hard day doing the lobbyist thing—or so she claimed—was leaned over the couch from behind, rubbing Sophie's neck. Sophie's neck didn't actually need rubbing, but it gave Penelope something to do besides work. "Is he as cute as Jon? How much time are you spending with him? What does he think Jon was up to? Is he single?"

"I want to hear what the cops are doing about this break-in." Jan tried to close up an overfilled box of books. "Foggy Bottom's supposed to be safe. The real thieves are supposed to be in DC—or on Capitol Hill—not here. It's scary. You want me to stay here for a few nights, Soph?"

"No, no, I'm fine. But I do appreciate all the help putting it back together. It would have taken me night upon night upon night." Sophie stood up, realizing all the knots in her neck were actually gone. "Thanks, Penelope. Man, are you great at that."

"I am," Penelope agreed with a frank laugh. "Men love a good back rub. It was a skill I acquired early. Anyway, you know what I heard?"

"What?" Jan's head popped up from her box.

"You know Athena Simpson? The woman senator from Arizona? I heard she broke down when she heard Jon died, closed up the office, just disappeared for a few days."

"But she's married," Sophie said.

Jan exchanged glances with Penelope.

"Cut it out," Sophie said crossly. "I know married people have affairs. It's just...she's a senator."

"Yeah, well, everyone says her husband's gay. Not bi. Gay. So I'm not throwing stones if she was sleeping with Jon on the side."

"I wasn't throwing stones," Sophie said. "I just..."

"You're just going to be naive until the day you die," Hillary said wryly, coming from the kitchen, wiping her hands on a towel. "You had your hard drive copied,

Sophie. Completely. And you had two corrupted files on there—but I don't think they were your work."

"You could fix the corrupted stuff?"

"Yeah, no sweat. In another life, maybe I'll do surgery on electronics instead of people. Although, really, Sophie, your backup procedures are first rate. You could have done this."

"Maybe," Sophie agreed. "But I thought it would help to have another set of eyes. When I went through it all my current work seemed to be there. And that's just it, why would someone mess with my computer system if they didn't take any of the work? For that matter, why would anyone look on here to begin with? Nothing I do is remotely top secret."

"Yeah, well, in Washington, even the whisper of something wicked is enough to start an avalanche."

"But not from me. No one could possibly think I was an avalanche starter— Cord!" All four women straightened at the sudden appearance of Cord in the doorway. "I thought you were teaching tonight," Sophie said swiftly.

"Canceled. In fact, I arranged for a free week, so I could concentrate on my brother's business. Ladies, I think I remember you all…Jan, Hillary, Penelope…"

Her heart seemed to hiccup. They'd shared kisses now. He'd slept in her room. They'd shared things, laughed together. She refused to be so preposterous as to believe it could be a love thing, but right at that instant, she knew she was in trouble. Heart trouble.

And before those idiotic allusions could seep under her defenses any deeper, she thought fate was helping her out. This was Cord's second shot at meeting the three women. He'd see how gorgeous they were. How…

brunette. How women-of-the-world. And then he'd stop looking at her as if...well, as if he were interested.

That's what she thought would happen. Yet, after a rapid round of hellos—and the women all inviting Cord to stay and share some pizza, as if this were their apartment—Cord put up a hand. "I don't want to interrupt. Unless you specifically want some help, Soph, I'll be next door. And I'll catch up with you whenever you have a chance."

When he disappeared across the hall, the women spun around to examine Sophie as if she'd suddenly grown two heads. "What?" she demanded.

"I saw the way he looked at you," Penelope said. "You've been holding out on us, girl. Let's hear it."

"Hear what?"

Hillary's jaw dropped. "You got involved with him? I can't believe it!"

"Wait, wait..." Sophie put her hands on her head. Only near Washington could the whisper of a rumor get out of control so fast. "Are you guys crazy? Why would someone like Cord look at anyone like me? The only reason we've talked is because of his brother. It's nothing personal."

Twenty minutes later the women left, carrying bags with leftover pizza and soda and anything else Sophie could force in their hands for a thank-you. In the sudden silence after their departure, she called for Caviar. The place looked almost like normal. The landlord would have to decide what he wanted to fix or replace, but her stuff was livable again. Almost every sign of the break-in had been whisked away

She felt safe again—life safe. Heart safe was a different story entirely, but she figured the only way to resolve that was to face it head-on.

Seconds later, Caviar next to her, she rapped on Cord's door.

He opened it as if he'd been waiting just on the other side. "I was hoping you'd have a chance to pop in. Nice of your friends to come over and help. Do you still have stuff you need doing?" He looked at her, then at the cat streaking past his legs. "Where's he going?"

"It's in pretty good shape. The girls were whirlwinds. And you've got enough on your plate without adding my messes to it. As far as where Caviar's going…my guess is, to the litter box."

"Why mine instead of yours?" he asked mournfully, clearly hoping to elicit a chuckle, but right off the bat, she could see he was distracted. "I told you I was taking that money to the authorities, which I did. I just wanted to fill you in on how that went, but…"

"What?" Maybe she'd come over because she'd promised to help with his brother's stuff. Maybe she just wanted to prove to herself that she could reduce the chemical pull around Cord by just behaving sisterlike with him. One millisecond, and that plan got jettisoned. Something was wrong. Not the wrongs of last week. A new wrong. She could see it in his face.

"I found some more stuff. In fact, I figured out—just in the last few minutes—exactly how my brother was making a living."

"So spill."

Sophie automatically pushed off her shoes at the door, but she couldn't take her eyes off him. Forget risk. Forget what she shouldn't be feeling. Cord had been fine when he stopped by, yet now he gave off tension, as if he'd been slapped with a live electric wire. She glanced around, trying to pick up clues about what he'd been doing.

Apparently, he'd been sitting on the carpet in the living room. A tall glass sat on the coffee table, still loaded with melted ice cubes, nothing but a leftover acrid aroma to tattletale the scotch he'd been drinking. She suspected he'd chugged it, or the cubes wouldn't still be there. A dozen CDs were strewn in front of the flat-screen monitor, but just then, the screen was black.

Instinctively, she aimed for the mess on the floor and crouched down. "Okay, what are these CDs?" she asked.

He didn't directly answer, just hustled to push the CDs into a box behind him before dropping to the carpet next to her. And then he started talking, but not totally making sense. Man, he was wiped, she thought. Heart wiped. Soul wiped.

"My parents," he started, and then just heaved out a gruff sigh. "I can't say enough about them. They were both so…decent. So totally good people. They believed in crappy old-fashioned ideals, like integrity and honor and loyalty. In their lives, certain things were automatic…like shoveling out their neighbor's drive after a snowstorm, and church on Sunday, and taking a neighbor food when they were sick. Growing up, I never thought about any of that. It's just how it was, how they were. We weren't fancy people. Just good. All the way to the bone."

She waited. He scrubbed his forehead like he was trying to erase strain lines etched in ink. "I left. I mean, for God's sake, I was grown-up. It was time I made my own way. But I admit, I couldn't wait to get out of town, make a life of my own. I did the military thing, then to the State Department—was overseas for long months at a time. I didn't get home often. Just couldn't. When you're young and dumb and busy saving the world, you assume everything'll be the same when you get back. They knew I loved them. I knew they loved me. All that crap." He looked up suddenly. "Hell, I'm going on like a runaway train. Didn't even offer you a dri… Oh. Well, maybe best not to offer you liquor, huh, Big Drinker?"

She liked the teasing. Maybe too much. "Shut up, Cord. And no, I don't need anything, alcoholic or otherwise. But you want another?" She motioned to his glass.

"No."

He couldn't seem to get talking again, so she pushed. "What's on the CDs?"

And that set him off again, although not directly answering her question. "My mom got cancer. I came home. Pretty sure I told you that before. All along, they hadn't told me what trouble Jon had been, what trouble he was into. I mean, Jon was *born* a handful, but I didn't know how bad things had gotten until I got home, and then I could see my parents were…gray. Gray with worry, gray with fear. Not drugs. That was one thing they didn't seem to be afraid he was doing. But Jon… He was so good-looking, so full of charm that he always seemed to squeeze out of trouble. He never wanted to think he was like everyone else. He didn't want to work. He didn't want responsibility. Yet he wanted *something* all the time. As if some kind of hunger was eating him up from the inside. Nothing respectable ever seemed to ring his chimes."

When Cord again fell silent, Sophie figured the elephant in the room had been ignored for long enough. "So it's porn on the CDs?"

The way he looked at her was answer enough. And then he sprang to his feet as if he couldn't sit still any longer. Caviar ambled in and crouched down by the fireplace, his eyes at a lazy half-mast, but Sophie thought the old tom had adopted Cord. Or maybe battered males just tended to stick together, who knew?

Cord prowled the room like a scarred-up old cougar, punching a button here, a switch there…a mistake to do in his brother's living room, where out of nowhere firelight or sexy music or sexy dim lights could suddenly change the landscape.

He switched off whatever he switched on, but it was obvious he wasn't paying attention. And though Sophie listened to his words, she paid the most attention to his body language and expressions. He hated it, she thought. Pride was the problem. He hated talking about issues that shamed him, that ripped open his sense of honor—at least as he saw it.

"You know, I wouldn't give a damn if it were just porn. The first CD I came across, I just thought the film was, you know, lovers, playing games, filming each other. Lovers do such things. Not up to me to be their judge and jury. Only, damn it, this wasn't about lovers. Because each CD has a different name or initial on it. There's 'HS' and 'Janella.' 'MM.' 'AFB,' 'Penny, Bel.' I stopped counting, but there have to be twelve different names. None of the CDs are dated, so I don't know how old these are, what year, any information like that. The first one I saw, though—I recognized her from the news, she's one of the local anchors in the morning. Damn it, she's got two young kids."

She searched his face. "As upsetting as this is, Cord… none of this is your shame or your blame. It's on your brother. And on the women he got involved with."

"I just don't get how he turned out so…crooked. Maybe if I'd been here more—"

"You were the younger brother, right?"

"Yeah, but I was always stronger than him. And when I left, I was thinking about myself, my life, not what my parents were left to cope with. He was out of control a long, long time ago." He ran a hand through his hair. "Another face on a CD was someone in the Defense Department. Not high up, but still, hell, if he was blackmailing her, it could have been for more than money. The whole thing is—"

Slowly she stood up, not sure what she intended, but driven by some primal female instinct. It didn't take brilliant intuition to know, positively, that Cord didn't do emotional spills. He didn't live the kind of life where he ever expected to find himself knee-deep in muck, at least this kind of unethical, ugly muck. It wasn't his fault; it wasn't his doing, but responsibility still showed in every forehead crease, every pinch around his eyes, every stiff-shouldered movement.

She knew about that.

She knew about feeling alone, about being alone, about trying to build a shell around herself so thick that hurt couldn't get through.

She knew about wading through mud, trying to find a way that would make sense, willing to do anything, to be anything, to turn herself into someone else, if that's what it took to survive.

Cord frowned and stopped prowling around the room when he noticed her silently walking toward him.

As if suddenly uneasy, his hand seemed to unconsciously jerk on a switch. Lights dimmed, although he didn't seem aware of it. When she kept approaching him, he looked at her with a questioning expression.

"What's wrong?" he said.

And then she kissed him.

## *Chapter 6*

The minute Sophie roped her arms around him, she knew this was right.

Possibly, it was the scariest, stupidest, craziest thing she'd done in years—especially for a woman who hated risk.

But it was still right.

Cord was breaking. She suspected he saw himself as a tough, strong loner, because he was. But this crisis with his brother had started seeping through the cracks, threatening foundations. She'd had her own foundations threatened. She'd gotten lost in her own darned cracks.

That's why she had to do it. Kiss him and kiss him and kiss him.

When their lips first met, she felt the taste and smoothness and yielding of his mouth. Then, as if she'd shocked him beyond belief, his hands suddenly clenched her shoulders. He yanked his head back with an "Um, Sophie..."

She got the message from his gentle tone. She could get out of this. He'd make a gentle joke, and she could joke back, and they'd both be able to forget she'd acted like a crazy fool.

Instead, she went back up on tiptoe and absconded with another kiss. This time she framed his head in her hands and pulled him down to her height—or close enough.

Years ago, when she was still half a baby, she remembered belting out the blues from her front porch in her mom's high heels and a brush for a pretend microphone. That was before her world had broken. Before she'd broken.

All this time, that Sophie had been buried so deep that she'd never believed there was an inch of that wild girl left.

But it seemed there was...when she kissed Cord.

She still thought—knew—he wasn't being totally straight with her. She had no illusions or thoughts about a future or a capital-*R* relationship, or any of that nonsense.

But...somehow they seemed to be sharing something vulnerable and raw because of Jon. Things were coming out of his woodwork. Out of hers.

It wasn't a choice. It was what had been forced on them by life, by fate. But reaching out to him was still as necessary to her as breathing. She felt as if a primal life force were burgeoning up from some dark, dusty corner, seeking light, needing warmth. Cord had no reason to know that she never did this, that it was just too hard.

Yet with him…it was easy.

So, so, so easy.

He took over.

She should have known he would. Heaven knew, Cord wasn't a passive kind of guy. He may have been startled by that first kiss, particularly coming from her…but he turned on faster than whiplash.

Suddenly he wasn't just accepting her embrace, but doing the kissing, taking a whole lot of initiative. Long, sure hands stroked from her neck, down her spine, down to the swell of her fanny. He lifted her up, spun her, lips sealed, tongues finding each other like whispers in the night.

Her back thunked against a wall…not a hard thunk, but enough to make her exquisitely aware that Cord was losing control at rocket speeds. His keys definitely turned on her ignition. Her body instinctively arched against his. The heat of him enticed her heat; her breasts swelled for the rowdy desire now pulsing off him in waves.

"I don't know what's going on here," he whispered thickly against her throat, "but I know where it's going if you don't say stop damned quick."

"I don't want to stop. I want you."

Sophie knew she hadn't said that. Another woman in the room did. A stranger, a completely immoral, amoral stranger.

The same stranger pushed at his sweater, took his mouth as avidly, as hungrily, as he took hers. Beneath the wool was hair-roughened skin, the ripple of muscle and sinew, nothing soft. He was going to kill her, she figured. He was too big, at least for a woman her size, a woman who hadn't exactly done this…much less in recent history.

Almost in recordable history. And here she was, still yanking off the sweater, demanding bare flesh, needing to touch him. Everywhere. Anywhere. When he started chaining kisses down her throat, she nipped at his shoulder. Just little bites.

He tasted damn good.

"Jesus, where did all this come from?" he muttered. "I thought you were shy."

"I was." For years and years and years, she was. With other men, she was.

She reached around, felt his adorable, irresistible tight butt. Sheesh, how could he have those huge broad shoulders and no butt? She squeezed…which may have been a mistake, because one minute she was pressed up against the wall, and the next she was on the floor, her sweater being shoved over her head, his hands on his zipper before she could suggest…

Well…

"Condoms."

"As if I'd risk you," he said. "They're in my back pocket."

For a whole second she turned back into the *real* Sophie Campbell again and panicked. "Always prepared, huh? You have a lot of women suddenly spring themselves on you?"

"No, Sophie. And if they did, I wouldn't jump into a 'yes.' I'm saying yes to you. Just you."

*Well, hell…* She lost the careful, cautious, predictable Sophie and became that other woman again. She asked him other questions, but they were carnal questions, laced with teasing, spiced with enticement. Secrets. About what she was afraid was going to happen. About what she feared wouldn't.

He answered her with whisper, with touch. At the same time, he was peeling off the rest of her clothes, one garment at a time. Once the sweater was gone, he stroked his soft tongue down her throat, to the swell of her breasts, to the rim of a pink-and-black bra.

"Not what I expected," he murmured. "But then nothing I'm finding is what I expected about you, Sophie Campbell."

The black lace bra disappeared, replaced by his mouth, testing and tasting and exploring the territory revealed. Her nipples tightened until they hurt. The room...wasn't dark enough. Not for this. Not for the exotic road of his tongue, down to her navel, down, as his hands chased her slacks off, as if the silky heat of his tongue could cover where she was being uncovered.

She started shivering then, but not from cold. The look in his eyes was intent, intense, cherishing. She had an old fantasy about a lover who stole into her room in the night, who weaved a spell, seduced her, forced her to do brazen, abandoned things. It was her favorite fantasy.

This was better.

He was better. Better than a dream. Better than any lover she'd ever conjured up. He inspired her to feel... need. Desire, like an avalanche. Her own power and sensuality, as if she were meeting up with her own Armageddon. Or his.

He peeled her off the wall, scooped her up. "Say no," he whispered.

"Yes."

A kiss, swift, sure. God knew where he was walking with her. He didn't seem to know, either. The hall was dark. He never switched on a light, stumbled once—she thought they'd both crash and tumble. Instead, his knees connected with something, and then she bounced on the bed…and he bounced on her.

"Say no," he advised her, urged her, one more time.

"Yes." She twisted, until she was on top, bare. The mattress was hard, big as a room, the textures of down and chill-cool percale under her knees. But his body was warm, when she swooped down with hands and lips. His body, truth to tell, threatened to burn.

They roller-coastered together, playing tease, hide-and-seek, double dare. The room had no more light than charcoal dust—but his eyes picked up light, picked up her. Her laughter belled in the darkness, throaty, brazen….and his gruff chuckle turned into a roar when she accidentally tickled him.

She'd never heard him laugh before….not really laugh, not belly laugh. She couldn't remember the last time she'd let loose with abandoned laughter before, either. At that moment, though, she just wasn't Sophie. She was that wild girl that had been lost so long ago, never really gone, but just waiting for someone to turn the key on the rusty lock.

Cord had the key.

Cord *was* the key. Laughter died, the last time he knelt over her. She touched his face, invited with the shine of her eyes, and then arched her back helplessly when she felt his slow, deep intrusion. He filled her up, she wrapped her legs tight around him, and there it was, the gallop off into the sunset, on a ride as primal as heartbeats, as hope, as love.

"Yes," he whispered, just as he felt her last climb, her last spin of a climax. He was only a blink behind.

She wasn't aware of falling asleep, but the next time she opened her eyes, someone had transported her from Oz to reality. Defibrillators couldn't compete with this kind of jolt. She seemed to be snoozing on the cushy carpet in Jon's hall—how impossible was that? She also seemed to be naked as a jaybird—another shock. And most impossible of all, Cord was awake, lying just as naked as she was, balanced up on an elbow. Studying her.

The ambient light from some other room barely dented the dark hall. Still, there was enough for her to see Cord's expression. The look in his eyes made Sophie want to glance behind her, certain there must be another woman in the room somewhere—the one he was studying with that tender, mystified, intense gaze.

"I fell asleep?"

"Just for the last few minutes. I don't doubt you needed a nap to recover. Soph?"

"Hmm?" For just a moment, she forgot to be appalled and shocked at herself. He was so luscious naked. Not soft. Not pretty. But all those long, sinewy muscles and angles, all that rough hair, all that...*whew*. Her eyes shot back up to his. He'd caught where she was staring. His smile was full of male ego.

Still, he seemed determined to say a few serious things. He touched her cheek. "Do you have a clue what this was all about?"

"Well, I think it's called making love. It's been a while since I read the book my adopted mother gave me in fifth grade, but really, I'm pretty sure—"

A kiss shut her up, but he lifted his head immediately. Or almost immediately. "If you knew we were going to end up making love…I sure as hell didn't. I knew I was attracted. I knew the kick of hormones was damn hard to ignore. But I wouldn't have pounced, Soph, because I figured the last couple weeks were seriously traumatic for you. I don't like the idea of taking advantage of your vulnerability."

"You're not vulnerable?"

"Guys aren't vulnerable, didn't you know? Besides, for us, sex cures everything."

"Who knew?" she teased. But then she stopped kidding around and gave him a straight answer. "I didn't plan this. I didn't know or dream it was going to happen. And if you don't want it to happen again, it won't."

"Then it sure as hell will, because you won't find me saying no to a repeat of this, any time, day or night. Sophie…"

She didn't know what he intended to say, but her heart rate instinctively started slamming. If he didn't want to be with her in a more serious way, that would be unsettling and hurtful. But if he *did* want to be with her, that had some unexpected and scary implications, too.

Trying not to look as if she were suddenly in a blister of a hurry, she stood up and forced a quick laugh. "I see Caviar from the top of the couch, looking at us."

"A voyeur cat?"

The mild diversion broke the intensity. A little awkwardly, she started reaching for her clothes—although she seemed to have forgotten where a few key items had landed. Still, she found her pants, found her bra, managed to cover herself.

"Um, Soph, if you were thinking about going back to your apartment tonight…it's not happening."

"I have a really early—"

"Yeah, I know that excuse. I usually have a 'really early' thing, too. Sometimes it's even true. But you're not going next door tonight, not after that break-in. My brother, God love him, has the best mattress I've ever been near—so heaven knows why we ended up on the floor. But I guarantee that a nice warm bath in his shamelessly sybaritic bathroom will make you sleepy. Particularly if you drink a glass of wine while you're soaking. And then we'll fold you into that big, fabulous bed."

"Are you trying to make me an offer I can't refuse?" Her voice was petulant.

"Damn right."

"And is part of that plan sleeping together in that alleged big, fabulous bed?"

"Yeah, it is. But we can adjust that part of the plan, if you've got a concern with it."

"I don't. I just wanted to be sure we were talking the same language," she assured him. Heaven knew how that came out of her mouth. It wasn't remotely true. She wasn't talking Cord's language in any conceivable way.

Serious shock was sinking in. Her pulse was thudding with it, her heartbeat as skittery as a doe in the rutting season. All these years, she'd been a quiet, studious, cautious, ace-the-course good girl.

The Sophie she used to be—the girl-child Sophie, the selfish, fearless and uninhibited little girl—Cord had brought her out. The Sophie she once was. The woman she thought she'd turn into once upon a time—the kind of a woman who reveled in her sensuality, in her power with a man, trusting him at her most vulnerable moments...because she could. And still be safe.

Only in real life, Sophie knew better than to run with scissors.

She wasn't as safe as she'd been that morning, not because of the break-in, but because of Cord. Being with him had ripped off layers that she'd counted on being glued tight. So she knew now...he was dangerous.

Deliciously dangerous, but it wasn't so delicious to discover that she was dangerously vulnerable with him.

After the bath—in a tall malachite tub with seductive lighting and built-in music—she trekked around until she found Jon's bedroom. As she could have expected, Jon had gussied it up the same way he had the rest of the place. Platform bed. Mirrors. Black sheets. Corny and dumb, but man.

When she climbed into that bed, the mattress really *was* incredible.

Not as incredible as the naked man in it, but still breathtakingly incredible.

"I get the left side," she told him.

"We could flip a coin for it."

"Or you could give in."

"Or I could give in," he agreed, scooched over and pulled up the down comforter, offering her an invitation to slide in closer.

As soon as she switched off the light, she did.

In the suddenly fuzzy darkness, he said, "Am I sleeping with the librarian Sophie or the Lorelei seductress?"

"The librarian. It's possible the seductress could

again show up tonight. But not yet." She punched the pillow, fussed and curled and uncurled until she had it all right, her cheek on the pillow facing him, her neck covered up. For some crazy reason, she reached out for his hand.

Found it.

And she talked to him like that. Holding hands. As if they were kids just falling in love.

"Cord," she said, softly, seriously. "Your brother's death wasn't accidental. I don't care what the police or coroner or anyone else told you. It wasn't accidental. It just couldn't be."

It took a moment before he responded. "I know."

"My place wasn't broken into by chance, either. It was about Jon. It *had* to be about Jon."

Again, he responded slowly. "I came to the same conclusion."

"A lot of women could want those CDs. In fact, I'd think every single woman in each of those films would want her CD."

"That's exactly my take on the problem, too."

She felt the warmth of his palm against the warmth of hers. His touch was tender, sure. She fought to stay on track. "I don't know what you plan to do with those CDs. I guess you'll feel you have to give them to the police. But your brother's killer won't necessarily know that they aren't still in this apartment."

He loosened a hand, lifted it to brush a strand of hair from her cheek in the darkness. This time, he didn't waste breath verbally agreeing. They both knew it was true. So she just finished up what she needed to say.

"So...for me to be safe. For you to be safe. For us to get our lives back—we have to know who killed your brother. We have a *why.* The films and photos Jon took are a clear-cut *why.* But all of those women aren't murderers. Only one. The rest of them are victims. Victims who are so scared of exposure, so desperate that they could keep trying to find ways into this building to find Jon's blackmail stash."

"You're thinking the same way I've been," Cord agreed.

"There has to be more than those CDs to find. Records, names, addresses. So let's start exploring. Both of us. I'll help you look, any way I can. I don't understand why the police didn't uncover more of this themselves, but the bottom line is that it doesn't matter. The only thing that matters is that the killer is found as soon as possible."

*And then,* Sophie thought, *I'll be safe again.* The threat of Jon's murderer would disappear. The rest of the CDs and evidence could be destroyed. And Cord would leave. Whatever had sparked this tempestuous fire between them, she had no idea, but she couldn't imagine his thinking of her as a long-term relationship. They barely knew each other. She had no excuse for fantasizing along those story lines, either.

So it wouldn't be the same thing as abandonment. As having her heart ripped out of her chest. Not if she knew this wasn't permanent, that it couldn't possibly go on too long.

"Soph," he murmured. "We can't solve any more of this tonight."

"I know," she agreed.

"So let's see if we can inspire that wild, uninhibited Sophie to come out of hiding for just a little longer..."

He leaned over her, his gaze caressing her in the darkness, and then dipped down.

He claimed later that she swept him under, but Sophie didn't care who did the sweeping. She didn't care about all the "no matter whats." This moment, this man, was everything that could possibly matter. She couldn't imagine regretting anything about being with him.

In the middle of the night, she felt a soft *oomph* at the foot of the bed. A moment later, Cord murmured groggily, "There damn well better not be a cat on this bed."

Sophie opened an eye, saw the glitter of Caviar's collar and heard the tom's thunderous purr as the feline settled between them, protecting both in the night.

Cord woke up to the howl of an angry wind and the thwack of branches against the windows. Wet leaves would make the roads slick as grease. A far better morning to stay curled up with a slight blonde snuggled next to him…but Sophie was gone. With the damned cat.

He hopped in the shower, uneasily aware that he already missed her. She had to work, of course, and so did he, but that wasn't the point. She was a woman he wasn't supposed to trust.

Before he'd finished negotiating with his brother's coffee machine, his cell phone buzzed. Like a slap of reality, the caller was the detective, Bassett. For a few hours, Cord had managed to forget the porn CDs, the murder, his brother's unforgivable choices. "Yes, I left a message for you and Mr. Ferrell last night. And yes, I have some information for you, but I also have two classes this morning. The soonest I can shake free is around one."

"That's fine. Where?"

Cord thought, then picked one of the fast-eat places in the Smithsonian. It was neutral ground, easier for him to hike from the metro, and a fast route back to his brother's place.

He got there early, copped a sandwich and a pastry, found a seat where he could watch the entrances—and then couldn't eat. He didn't want to be here, talking to the cops. Questions and issues were going to come up about Sophie—questions and issues he had no answers for.

Replays from last night had lingered in his mind all morning, fragile as silken cobwebs, magical as moonlight. A while back, Sophie had told him she couldn't feel safe if she thought someone was going to disappear on her. The comment stemmed from her feelings about losing her parents. She'd felt abandoned, lost, alone. She'd learned young not to open the trust door. It was easier to keep the door shut than to risk being abandoned again.

Cord had nothing like that in his background—except for Zoe. And Zoe had taught him precisely the same lesson. He thought he'd gotten the right woman, a woman who'd stand by him—and then: zap. First taste of serious trouble, she's gone. He hadn't opened the trust door since.

Until Sophie.

A gaggle of women passed, all headed for the gem exhibit. Everyone coming in was shaking off rain, groaning about the ornery weather. Cord picked up his sandwich, then put it down.

His heart somehow started trusting Sophie, almost from the beginning. But everything about last night had been...startling. Beyond fantastic, but still startling. Who could possibly have guessed that beneath those god-awful clothes and oversize glasses was a sensual seductress who bared all and invited even more? When had he ever found a woman who seduced his head as much as his body, who made his blood run hot—and who confused the holy hell out of him?

Abruptly, he saw both Ferrell and Bassett, as noticeable in the sea of tourists as apples in a barrel of oranges. They wore similar rain gear, carried similar mugs of coffee, had that ill-fitting suit-coat thing going on. Both of them shook off their wet trench coats, didn't waste time, took seats on both sides of him.

Cord filled them in immediately about the CDs he'd found, how his brother had them hidden, behind the back wall of a cabinet drawer.

"Thank God," Bassett said. "That's exactly the evidence we needed. How many were there? Did you bring them all?"

"No." He added carefully, "I'm not certain that I'm willing to turn them over."

"That isn't a choice you get to make." The jowly detective took a pull from his coffee. "That's evidence, cut-and-dried. The concrete link we need to connect the killer to your brother."

"I know." Cord had thought it through all morning. "I don't think there's any question that the killer is connected to these home videos—either on the video, or a relative of one of the women. But it isn't that simple to me."

"It's very simple." Heat climbed Bassett's neck, turned his complexion dark.

Cord said slowly, "The problem with turning over all of those CDs is that those CDs would then be public. I'd be happy if I knew which one was connected with my brother's death. But I don't. And my brother apparently did a fine job of threatening a lot of lives and reputations. There's a lot of scandal in those films. Making them public could ruin a lot of people—without necessarily telling us who the killer was, or how relevant that evidence is to convicting the killer."

Before Bassett could suffer an attack of apoplexy, Ferrell leaned forward, with his usual amiable, calm expression. "I'd feel exactly as you do. Unfortunately, you have to trust someone with this evidence. It doesn't solve anything for you to keep those CDs to yourself."

"Believe me, I have no interest in keeping them—"

Bassett interrupted, all but snapping and yapping. "That's good, because you're not. You just keep in mind that I could lock you behind bars in two seconds if I needed to. You're not going to get away with impeding an ongoing investigation. I'll charge you with obstruction so fast it'll make your head swim."

Thinking about Sophie, Cord hadn't been able to eat. Dealing with a simple legal crisis, he reached for his sandwich again. "But you're not going to do that," he said calmly, "because you know perfectly well I've cooperated. And that I'll continue to help. The only place I'm drawing the line is where innocent people could be hurt by this mess."

"Come on, Pruitt. No one on those CDs is anywhere near a definition of *innocent*."

The ham on rye was going down pretty well. "There's a lot of miles between murder and someone behaving immorally, or making a mistake." Cord unfolded a strip of paper from his shirt pocket. "These are the initials or words that were on each CD. There were no full names and dates. But take a look."

The two of them fell on the list faster than rabid dogs, enabling Cord to finish his lunch. Tourists ambled by in bunches, speaking every language on the planet, stopping for snacks between exhibits. Cord kept thinking that Sophie would really get off on this. The exhibits, the history. Everything about the Smithsonian. And for darn sure, all the people-watching potential.

All too soon, the men returned their attention to him. They had become subdued in those few minutes. Bassett was the first to speak. "No way to be positive of anything from this little amount. But I suspect who the MM is. The wife of a senator on the Appropriations Committee."

Cord winced. "Not good."

"Definitely not good to imagine that video loose in the media. Also damn easy to imagine someone motivated to do anything—maybe even murder—to get that CD."

"That one, you can have."

That was exactly what Cord had been hoping to hear. "This just *has* to be a quid-pro-quo deal. If you can just verify that you have knowledge or suspicions about anyone linked to those words, then I'll immediately give you the applicable CDs."

Bassett wasn't through. "At least one other name

springs out at me. Penny. That could well be a nickname for Penelope Martin. She's a lobbyist for some kind of legal rights group. I believe she's also a friend of your brother's neighbor, Sophie Campbell."

Cord felt a fast chill chase down his spine. "Sophie has nothing to do with this."

Bassett rolled his eyes. "You know this how?"

"Because I've been around her now. I *know* her."

"You don't *know* her. You've been around her for a few days. Somehow, she's miraculously been around a lot of people involved in this case. Penelope Martin is paid a damn good salary to swing senators' votes. She's slept her way to influence before this. Now we find out she was sleeping with your brother, too."

"Since you're already aware of that, I'll be happy to turn over that CD to you. As well as the MM one."

For the first time, Ferrell leaned forward, as if finally engaged in the conversation. "This is good evidence, Cord, but it's not enough to convict or even arrest anyone. We still need you to watch Sophie. We still have every reason to believe she's connected to this. Your so-innocent Sophie befriended at least one potential suspect in the case that we know of, and possibly more. Someone clearly believes she knows something important, or her place wouldn't have been broken into. A lot of things point to her as having ink stains on her character."

"It's not her," Cord repeated.

"We're just asking you to stay alert. To keep looking, keep listening. We're still in the middle of all this—there's DNA coming back, prints, hopefully more evidence to uncover from the money you turned over, and we still don't have the test results from the autopsy.

She's not the only person we're looking at, but she's still in the picture. Still part of the problem."

"I'm not having this conversation again with you guys. I won't spy."

"We've been through this before," Bassett said. "You don't need to use that three-letter word if it puts your Jockeys in a twist. Just...be a team player. We all want the same thing. To find out who killed your brother."

Minutes later, when Cord pushed open the door, in a hustle to get away from them and out of there, the stormy morning had intensified. Rain poured down in slashing, slapping sheets, kicking branches and leaves and debris everywhere. It was only a short hike to the metro, but long enough for him to get chilled to the bone.

Cord didn't need a PhD to realize Bassett and Ferrell wanted something a lot bigger than his brother's murderer. That was a given. Get near politicians and money and power in Washington, and ambition for more was always the story. He didn't care what their problem was—and for damn sure, he didn't care what their scandal was.

But the connection to Sophie gnawed on his nerves with sharp teeth. He'd told them flat out that he refused to spy on her. But the reality was that he *did* need to stay close to Sophie—for her sake. To protect her. Because for damn sure the cops wouldn't, as long as they believed she was on the wrong side of this story.

Neither Ferrell nor Bassett, of course, would believe that any time Cord spent with Sophie was for her sake. They'd think he was playing ball.

He *was* playing ball.

Just not in their court.

Only every minute since his brother was killed—ever

since he met Sophie—he felt more and more as if he were tiptoeing on a high wire. And his feet were a clumsy size twelve.

## *Chapter 7*

All day, Sophie felt akin to the circus acrobat who had to balance on a high wire.

No matter what she tried to do, fate seemed to yank her off balance in an unexpected direction. Obviously, she'd had no choice to leave Cord this morning and go to work, but her interview with Inger Henriks was originally only scheduled for two hours. Instead, it had dragged on for five.

"My family," Inger had told her, "they were always saving the American fliers. Flyboys, we called them in the war. Our house was in the harbor, Helnaes Bugt. That was the thing. You know, Denmark has a border with Germany. So the flyboys would come in the dark, run out of fuel, drop in the water like flies. We'd fish them out, feed them, hide them. Did the Swedes do this? Did the Finns? No. It was us, the Danes. Always us. I was proud of this, we all were, but still. I was just a child. We had this dangerous secret in our lives, where if anyone had overheard us whispering, we could be caught. My family were fishermen. And I was just a girl who wanted to believe in fairy tales and dreams. Instead, I was afraid every day. Secrets—this is no way to live."

The stories had gone on and on—each of them heart-touching, compelling and powerful. If it weren't for Cord, she'd have been thrilled to spend the extra hours. She loved her job, especially loved this project, and felt enriched by every one of the elderly women she'd had a chance to interview.

It was just…there *was* Cord. Also a murder and the break-in and the mess of blackmail Cord's brother had been involved with—but that stuff was just, well, danger. Troubling and scary and all, but hardly as momentous as making love with Cord last night.

Nothing could be that momentous. Not for Sophie.

She couldn't get home until midafternoon, and by then she was frazzled, soaked from the mean, cold rain and out of breath. Cord wouldn't be there until later. The plan was to scour Jon's apartment, open every ceiling tile, pat down every floorboard. But she had much to do before then—starting with changing clothes, copying her interview tapes to her home system and buckling down to some serious translating work.

Her cell phone rang before she'd even taken off her coat…and Caviar was all over her with demanding meows. The cat had something shiny in its mouth—a trophy, like a bottle cap—and clearly wanted her to value the treasure. Sophie tried yanking off her jacket, petting Cav and responding to her sister at the same time.

"I haven't talked to you in a week, and I've been worried to bits about how you're doing. I was out on the water and just couldn't get a connection." Cate's voice was as forceful and vibrant as Sophie's was soft.

Cate was thirty, and had carved out a career as an adventure chef, which meant, as far as Sophie could tell, that her sister got to travel to every exotic place on the planet. Cate had cooked her way from Madagascar to Antarctica to halfway up Everest—rough-and-tumble places that Sophie had never gone or aspired to go to. But that was Cate. "You sound different from last week," her sister said suspiciously.

"Well, I'd hope so. I was a wreck when I talked to you last. I'd just found my neighbor's body."

Cate listened to the latest rundown of events, but then interrupted again. "There's still something different in your voice. There couldn't be something really unusual in your life—like a man—could there?"

"No. Well, yes. I mean, not exactly…." Sophie wanted to stare at the phone in exasperation. How was it her sister could smell a rose in a patch of peonies? "Yes, there's a man in my life, but it's not how it sounds. He's related to my neighbor. So it's not as if we met in the usual way."

"Soph, if you waited to meet guys in the usual way, you'd be a virgin at ninety-five. Like your current work project. You talk to old ladies and spend the rest of the time huddled in front of a computer. Guaranteeing you won't meet any men."

"That's so unfair. And untrue," Sophie began. She tried to sit, but Caviar climbed on her lap, tried to cuddle under her neck, batted her face when she failed to give him her complete attention.

"Just tell me straight. How far has it gone?" Cate waited all of three seconds, and when Sophie didn't respond that fast, she burst out, "Well, hell, *that* far? You?"

"What do you mean, *me?* You've been known to leap into bed with a guy who rings your chimes."

"But that's me, baby. Not you." Cate dropped the teasing note altogether. "That's the thing, Soph. We're both always waiting for a fire. Waiting for our lives to blow up, in some way we can't possibly foresee or control. So I pick men for a day, never give them a chance to stay. And you steer clear of anyone you can feel close to. It's really the same coin, just two different sides of it. We're both always ready to have to jump out a window at a moment's notice. But suddenly you're coloring way, way outside your lines."

"I did. I admit it. It's probably nuts." And just when she was getting into a real heart-to-heart with Cate, the buzzer for the front door interrupted.

"I don't know whether it's nuts or terrific," Cate grumbled. "I just think I should fly over there. Anyone messing with my baby sister better know there'll be hell to pay if he hurts you."

"Cate. Come on. People get hurt all the time. It's life. Nobody can save anybody else that."

"Horse hockey. I'll strangle him if he isn't good to you. And damn it, I have to go—but I expect a complete report before next week. And I'm calling Lily, so she knows what's going on. What's this guy's name?"

Caviar tried to trip her en route to the door, and she almost dropped the phone. It would help if she weren't galloping. She hadn't expected Cord to get here until closer to the dinner hour, but just picturing him on the other side of the door had her pulse doing the jazz riff of a love song.

"Cord," she said automatically as she opened the door, only to find Penelope Martin there instead. She motioned her friend in, still trying to end the call and handle Caviar at the same time.

"I heard you say Cord's name," Penelope said a few minutes later as she made herself tea. "That's why I stopped by. Finished a little early on Capitol Hill, and I just kept thinking how troubling this has all been for you. I wondered if the police had any leads on the person who broke into your apartment."

The stop by was a surprise, but Sophie told herself she might have expected it. Penelope inhaled gossip the way an alcoholic buzzed for the scent of scotch, a requirement every day, more valued than air. As always, Penelope looked groomed to the gills, doing the navy and white thing today—except for the flash of red in her ears. Sophie suspected Pen would consider rubies a justifiable expense to enable the patriotic color scheme.

"The police haven't found a single thing?" Penelope echoed with total disappointment. By then they both had mugs of tea; Sophie had scrounged up some not-too-stale snickerdoodles and run in and out of the bedroom, shedding her flannel skirt for jeans and a black sweater. Only, then she decided to run back in and change her bra—not that she was certain something would happen with Cord tonight.

That reality suddenly drowned her upbeat mood. She really didn't know how Cord would greet her tonight.

How he'd feel about last night. How he'd feel about her. If he'd regret what happened between them.

"Sophie, you mentally wandered off again. Did you even hear me?"

Of course she'd heard Penelope. She was just too busy having a nervous breakdown to concentrate. And suddenly she was feeling particularly dumb and vulnerable because she'd changed to the yellow froth of a bra that she shouldn't have bought to begin with, it was that frivolous and sexy and silly and…

*"Sophie."*

And he'd probably take it as invitation. Which wasn't what she meant. Or maybe it was. She scraped back her hair, feeling completely exhausted. "I don't know what the police have found, Penelope. Except that I think Cord believes—and so do I—that his brother's death wasn't as simple as an accidental fall. He's been trying to go through Jon's apartment, but he's working, so he has to fit it in a few hours at a time. There's no way he can do it quickly."

"So…he's just getting started? Has he found anything good so far? You know what I mean. The scoop on Jon and his women and all the stuff we always talked about. Jan's been on pins and needles, wondering whether Jon kept something from the time they slept together."

Sophie started to respond, then hesitated. "For sure, there was nothing about Jan. Cord met Jan and you and Hillary that one time. So he knows we're friends, so I think he'd have mentioned it if he found something related to any of us. Otherwise, I don't know."

Caviar pawed at her knee, showing off some treasure of a toy again, giving her the excuse to drop her eyes. She felt bad, not being totally straight with Penelope.

A week ago, she'd have freely told what she knew. Now everything was different. It wasn't a matter of not trusting Penelope or anyone else. It was about fearing what the murderer believed—about Jon, about her, about Cord. About who really had access to the blackmail evidence—or thought they did.

Penelope sighed with disappointment and stood up. "Darn it. I was hoping you'd picked up more. You'd tell me if you found out anything, wouldn't you? You know…Jan always bragged about sleeping with Jon. But I'd feel bad if she somehow got hurt because of it. If you found out something, we could try to protect her."

"I'd hate to think of her getting hurt, too."

Penelope pulled on her coat. "I've made this sound like a selfish visit. You know I love scandal. But I was honestly worried about Jan. And much more, about you. That break-in was no small thing. Anytime you want me to stay with you, just give me a call. You still must be petrified."

Sophie didn't think she was suffering leftover symptoms from the break-in—until she almost jumped out of her skin when she heard the next rap on the door.

Penelope had been gone for more than a half hour by then, and Sophie had installed herself in front of her computer, saving—and double saving—the interview work she'd done that day. She was afraid to trust her hard drive or her backup. Afraid every time she heard a creak in the walls or a whistle of wind.

When she heard the second rap on the door, she thought: *It has to be Cord. So it's okay.*

Only, her heart was still thundering like a wild drum. Apparently, nothing was going to be "okay." Any sense of safety in her life, in her heart, had been frayed at the edges.

There was no "safe" anymore. She'd learned that at five years old. How could she have forgotten that?

When Cord charged up the stairs and thumped on Sophie's door, he was wound tighter than a violin string. The meeting with Ferrell and Bassett had been unsettling and tricky.

The problems with his brother kept becoming more complex, more ugly, more dangerous. Cord was a problem solver. Give him an avalanche or a fire or an accident, and he dove right in—no fear, no hesitation. It wasn't as if he liked trouble, but he thrived when he had something to *do.* This business of waiting and waiting and waiting for another axe to fall, another piece to fit in the blackmail puzzle, was grating on his nerves.

When Sophie didn't respond, he knuckled her door again, this time harder. He shifted his feet. Rolled his shoulders. His nerves sharpened another notch.

All day, he'd wanted to see her.

All day, he'd worried about seeing her. He had no idea—none—how she'd greet him. If she'd regret last night or be happy about it. If she'd want to talk about what it meant, or want to pretend it never happened. If she'd shy from him like a wary colt, or assume last night meant…what?

Hell, he didn't know what last night meant himself. He *knew* he was wary of trusting another woman since Zoe…but he'd sure as hell trusted Sophie last night, in every way a man can trust a woman. Whatever name you wanted to call it, Cord wanted her with him every night, all night, for as long as she was willing.

Still…that didn't absolve him of responsibility for what his brother had gotten Sophie embroiled in. Cord had only put her in a more dangerous position since Jon's murder. Bottom line was that, if *he* were Sophie—he'd kick him out of her life so fast, it'd make his head spin.

When she didn't respond to the second knock, he frowned and rapped one more time—about to start getting damn worried—when Sophie suddenly yanked open the door.

Whatever he'd expected or been braced for, it wasn't a flying blonde.

She almost knocked him over. Damn woman leaped, slapped her arms around his neck and then just hung there, holding tight. Not breathing. Not speaking. Not moving. Just holding.

He closed his eyes, inhaled her scent, the tickle of her hair, the warmth of her body. Crazy as it sounded, that's all he needed or wanted to do for those moments. Hold her. Just like this. Eventually, though, his vocal cords functioned enough to say, "Not having the best day, huh?"

"Awful." Finally, she lifted her head, released him from that gluelike clutch hold. "I wasn't going to do this."

"Do what?"

"Say hi this way. I don't want you to think I'm a clinger. Or a chaser. But the thing is…you've probably had an awful day, too."

"You've got that right."

"And it's because of Jon. Or connected to Jon."

"Right again."

"So, who else can we possibly hug about this except each other?"

"This is about hugs, is it?"

Her cheeks flushed like a child's. So it wasn't about hugs. For her or him. And maybe she wasn't all that easy with last night, but her eyes still met his squarely, flush or no flush. She wasn't denying what happened between them. Or trying to.

She wasn't denying wanting him, either.

Although she did suddenly ease away. "Hey. No diversions until we get some work done. We need answers. We need information. This limbo land of waiting for the next crisis to get heaped on our heads is hugely not fun."

"We also need food."

"Well, yeah."

He had Thai delivered, her choice. It was clearly a favorite of both hers and Caviar's, since the cat hung over the edge of the computer desk, occasionally trying to bat the chopsticks from her hand. Worse yet, Sophie shared. With the cat.

How could he possibly be involved with a woman who shared Thai with a cat?

Out of the complete blue, words came out of his mouth that he never planned. "I was involved before."

"Yeah?" She lifted her eyes to his immediately, which gave the cat the opportunity for an extra steal.

He stood up, bunched up the napkins and boxes and debris. His voice came out light, easy, like he was telling her about the weather. "Yeah. Zoe. That was her name. Closest I came to marriage. In fact, we'd have been married if both of us hadn't had a lot of travel with our work, so we hadn't yet pinned down a date. Anyway. It was when my mother got sick. I quit the job and moved back here. She didn't like that, and that was that."

Soph rose, too, and dove into the cleanup with him. "If she hurt you, she's dead to me."

*Of all the crazy things to say,* he mused. But he didn't go on. He hadn't known he was going to even mention Zoe. And after that, they both dove into their attack plan for the evening.

The plan, simply, was to follow the money. Couldn't have been more trite or stereotypical, but hell, that was because it generally worked. The police believed they'd been through Jon's records from every possible angle already—but Sophie figured she'd look at the numbers from a female perspective, and immersed herself in front of Jon's computers.

Cord parked himself on the floor with boxes of old records. The cat, for no known reason, chose to sidle next to him. At least a half hour passed before either of them spoke.

"Cord?"

"Hmm." God. What his brother had spent on himself and pleasure boggled the mind. And where and how Jon could afford it all made Cord even more uneasy.

"Did you check Jon's mailbox today?"

"No. But I will right now." He jumped up immediately. Sitting still that long was straight torture. And since he had that outstanding excuse to move, he stalked behind her and dropped a kiss on the back of her neck—that spot with the down-soft hair and the silky white skin.

"Do *not* seduce me now," she complained.

He hadn't been. At least not exactly. He just couldn't get that "if she hurt you, she's dead to me" out of his head. It was so like Sophie to spill out her heart in a single, bold stroke.

He hustled downstairs and scooped the junk from the mailbox, started sifting through it all on the climb back up. Catalogs. Bills. More bills. Junk mail. And then… an envelope with a Cayman Islands address. A bank. It stopped him dead.

When he came back into the apartment, the darn cat—of course—tried to trip him. He was batting around a rolled-up piece of paper as if it were the best toy a human had ever given him. "Sophie?" How long had he been gone? Three minutes, four? She was no longer sitting in the computer room, although the printer was spewing out a long sequence of sheets.

He found her in the kitchen, crawled up on the counter, looking in the back of the top cupboard—heaven knew why.

"What's wrong?" he asked immediately.

"I found something. Something not good."

One short glance, and he could see her complexion had gone from healthy pink to chalk. "What?"

"I'll tell you. Right away. But sit down. I'm looking for whiskey or scotch or something."

"Another drinking night?" he murmured.

"For you, not me. I just made myself tea."

As if to illustrate the point, the microwave pinged. He plucked out her mug. For him, she pulled out a bottle of Talisker from the top shelf, opened it, reared her head away, as if the smell alone could give her sunburn, and scrambled in the cupboards for a glass. By then, she'd leaped back down to the floor and served him the drink—raw, no ice, no water.

"That might be a little strong," he mentioned.

"Trust me. You'll need it all."

"I found something, too. Something not so good, either."

"Wait!" She held up a hand like a traffic cop. "I need my bracer of tea first. How bad's your news?"

"Bad."

"Well, mine's worse. Mine is so bad that, if I were next door, I'd be cracking open the whole box of Oreos."

Damn, but she was forcing him to smile. He didn't doubt she'd found something troubling. He knew he had. But being with her could probably make hell almost better.

"Okay," she said and gulped a sip of tea. "I'm ready."

So he spilled his first. "My brother received an accounting from an offshore bank. It doesn't mention the account amount. It wouldn't. It just reports what he earned in interest for the last three months."

"This is scary?"

"I'd say ten thousand bucks—over that short period of time, for one account—is on the road to damn scary."

She took another gulp. "You don't suppose he just had a really high-yielding CD?"

Double damn, but he had to laugh. And she knew he couldn't help it, because she smiled right back at him. "So," she said cheerfully, "it looks as if Jon had been thriving in his blackmail career for quite a while. It's not everyone who has that kind of job skill, Cord."

"Trust you to see the positive."

"Hey, at least he was good at it. Money seems to be showing up all over the place around here." She braced, then clunked down her tea. "Okay. My turn. I was following the money, as we talked about. Going through the list of accounts in Jon's Quicken. I can't imagine he'd use an open program like that if he was trying to hide anything, so it was just as unlikely the police thought anything looked suspicious. And maybe they were right. But I found a payment of fifteen hundred dollars a month for the last eighteen or nineteen months to the same place."

"What was the name?"

"JONA."

Cord shook his head, mystified. "Doesn't mean anything to me."

"I'm not through." Her tone softened, the humor gone. "Once I pinned that down, I went back to when this all started. Around eighteen months ago, Jon paid a ton of credit card bills to various stores."

"Nothing odd about that."

"These stores were, like Toys 'R Us. A furniture store specializing in baby furniture. Several hundred dollars spent at another place, called Babies and Blankets."

"That doesn't make any sense." Cord frowned.

Since he wasn't drinking it, Sophie reached over, took his shooter of Talisker and threw back a slug. After another minute or two of violent coughing, she croaked, "I'm afraid it will. Wait a minute."

She charged back into the computer room and came back with her booty from the printer. The four pictures were grainy, poor-quality prints, but they illustrated the same thing—a baby. The first was a newborn shot, followed by a baby who was obviously a little older, and finally, a shot of a toothless, hairless, chubby-cheeked baby in a red-and-white Valentine dress.

"A baby," Cord said blankly. And without pause,

swallowed three solid gulps of the Talisker—a drink that deserved being savored with respect. "This can't be what it looks like. You're telling me my brother had a *baby?* On top of all the crap he pulled on people."

"I keep thinking that maybe there's some other explanation. But I can't think of one. He's been paying regular support, paid for a bunch when the baby was born. The pattern's pretty inescapable." Sophie studied the last photo, then said, "Looks as if you have a niece, judging from the dress."

Cord pushed away from the kitchen counter, the way a boxer might shoot off the ropes. "We're getting out of here."

"We are?"

"I've had enough. So have you. Enough of bad news and sad news. Enough of sleazy behavior and roads that lead to more sleazy behavior. Enough focusing on my brother."

"But, Cord, we've finally broken through, really started making some major discoveries. For the first time, I think we have a shot at figuring out the player, or players, in this whole mess. But maybe we should even be calling the police, telling them what we found out—"

"A lot of *shoulds* and *coulds* in that scenario. And I agree with you, Soph. But not right this second. Right this second, we're dumping this pop stand."

"Where to?" she asked bewilderedly.

# *Chapter 8*

Sophie was still trying to fathom it. How they'd ended up *here.*

She'd never been to Silver's before—never heard of it, and probably never would have, if Cord hadn't dragged her here. The place was stuffed with young professional people, even this late on a Thursday night. Most looked as if they'd come directly from their jobs, judging from the business suits on the men and the heels on the women, and typical of Washington, the buzz was all about the day's political events.

For an after-work hangout, the place struck Sophie as unusually appealing. The long bar gleamed under firelight and antique brass lanterns. Round mahogany tables were packed in tight, but a few revelers had left their seats, pushed off suit coats and kicked off heels, abandoned their drinks and hit the corner dance floor.

The music emanated from a new-fashioned jukebox—not the 50s era, art-deco type of box, but a brass-and-glass player with high-end speakers. Instead of quarters, the machine demanded bucks, and someone had emptied their pockets of singles to play a run of slow, bluesey love songs.

Those on the dance floor had abandoned politics, power and DC gossip. Tummies rubbed tummies. Arms hooked around necks. Cheeks rested against shoulders. Everybody wasn't addicted to stress, Sophie mused. Every once in a while, people actually remembered what life was really about.

Like falling in love.

Her mind wasn't remotely on the rest of the crowd, yet somehow she'd helplessly, hopelessly picked up the prevailing mood. Her arms, for instance, were roped under Cord's neck. Her cheek was definitely snuggled in the crook of his shoulder. Her tummy didn't happen to be rubbing against his tummy, because of the difference in their heights, but her tummy was unquestionably rubbing against his pelvis. Her breasts hummed awareness at the evocative contact; her pulse thrummed to the evocative beat of the song. If her eyes weren't smoky with shock, she thought they should be.

The shock wasn't finding herself in a place like this. The shock was that Cord had taken her here—apparently to dance. When he couldn't dance. At all.

He could make a girl fall in love, though.

Since Sophie didn't do reckless, didn't want to do reckless, had never remotely even felt reckless since she was five, she figured this had to be Cord's fault. She didn't rub her tummy against a guy's you-know-what. She didn't look up at him, nakedly communicating longing and desire. She didn't tease, with the graze of a breast, the tickle of a fingertip, the promise conveyed in the snuggle of body parts. She sure as Sam Hill didn't put up with a guy stepping all over her feet.

So there was only one conclusion she could possibly reach—that Cord had forced her, completely against her will, to feel this way.

"Are you thirsty?" she murmured. "We ordered drinks and then never even waited until they got to the table."

"Very thirsty. But not for drinks." He looked at her… as if he were a starving lion, and she was the only thing he hungered for. As if she were standing naked and he couldn't take his eyes off her. As if there wasn't a thought in his head but wanting her.

See, she told herself. It wasn't her fault little shivers kept chasing up her spine. It was all his.

"You don't think," she asked carefully, "that we should head home?"

"Hell, no. There's nothing waiting for us back there but more serious problems. More grenades without pins. We're not going home. Maybe ever."

"Um, Cord." She rubbed a finger on the nape of his neck. With her arms swooped protectively around him, she'd created a private cocoon between her face and his. Her eyes and his. She wasn't sure which one of them needed more protecting, but for darn sure, the expression on his face was stark with stubbornness. "They're going to close the place pretty soon."

"But not yet. It's not closing yet."

"Don't you have classes tomorrow?"

"Yup. An eight o'clock class, in fact. Don't care," he said; and then, as if all this talking had exhausted him, ducked down just those few more inches so his mouth could touch hers. Claim hers. Woo hers.

Her eyes closed. Plain old lust, she was positive she could have fought—or at least kept her head. But this cherishing, this tenderness, this wooing, was almost more than she could bear.

"I'm wondering," he murmured against her temple, "why I didn't realize how beautiful you were when I first met you."

"Because you were sober then?"

"I'm sober now. Which is why I have to be honest, and admit that at first I was fooled—by the bulky clothes and clumsy act and the glasses."

"I *am* clumsy. And I wear glasses."

"You wear very silly glasses," he said as he corrected her. "And you're not wearing them now. When I'm around you, you seem to forget to wear them more and more. Which tells me—"

"That I only need them for close reading?"

"Nope. It tells me that you don't feel you have to hide around me as much as you did before. And speaking of hiding, what kind of underwear are you wearing today?"

"I don't think I should answer that question."

"I think you should. I think it's a very important question. All we've been talking about for days are questions that aren't going to change the world. Questions that are disturbing and unsettling and ugly. Let's try to start this whole thing from the beginning, you and me. Let's just stick to the important questions. Like what kind of underwear you're wearing at this very minute."

"Yellow."

"Yellow?"

"Daffodil-yellow. White lace edges. I can't remember where or how it happened. But somehow en route, I got a little embarrassingly addicted to useless, pretty underwear."

"Don't even think about giving it up. This is probably the best addiction I've ever heard of. I think you should go with it. Forever."

"Um..." All right, her good sense and common sense had completely deteriorated, and she'd answered the underwear question. But one of them had to get a grip. Their tummies weren't just rubbing together. Their pelvises were locked tight. He was harder than petrified wood, and yeah, his erection was sealed against her, no one could see or know...but she knew. Fever shot through her bloodstream, making all that blood rush until she felt light-headed and dizzy.

"How come you don't tell me about your work?" he asked, out of the complete blue, as if they'd actually been having a serious conversation.

"Because I've never had a chance?"

"See? That's exactly the point I've been trying to make. All this crap with my brother has screwed up everything. We're not getting the chance to talk about what matters. What you do. Why you do it. Your yellow underwear. Your addictions."

"Cord?"

"What?"

"The music stopped playing. The bartender's wiping glasses. There are only two other people in the place."

"Hell, I don't see why it matters if there's music, when a person can't dance anyway," he remarked.

"Whew. I wasn't sure if you realized." Not that she

wouldn't dance with him again, Sophie mused. But the next time, she'd wear steel-toed shoes.

"You know what I *do* realize?"

"That we're going to get kicked out of this bar?"

"That you've never seen my place. It's a house. Rented, which isn't my choice, but I didn't buy when I first moved here. I wasn't sure how long I was going to stay. It's in Arlington, toward Falls Church. A drive, but I had to have some country, some trees, some green. And that's the thing. We can go there, to a place where we can both feel…clean. Away from the dirt around my brother's life. A place that's safe. A place where I can see that yellow underwear."

"I'd like to see it, Cord. But…I can't believe you'd feel…safe…leaving your brother's place completely deserted for the night."

"I wouldn't. But I keep trying to tell myself it doesn't matter. Someone breaks in, finds more answers, more stuff—why should this be any skin off *my* nose? I've been cleaning up my brother's messes since I was born. This one's making me sicker by the day. And I hate it. That you're close to it. At risk because of it."

"That's not your fault."

"Maybe not my fault. But it sure as hell feels like my responsibility."

"But that's only because you're stuck being one of those alpha guys, Cord. I totally understand that you can't help it. The only one who's really responsible for the mess is the mess maker. And that's Jon."

This hour, these last hours, he'd been so playful and crazy and fun. Seductive. Dangerous in the most seductive and luring of ways. But now he pressed his forehead into hers, said quietly, "Soph. I want you to leave town. Get away from this. You said you had two sisters. You could go visit one of them, at least for a couple weeks. Until this is…safe."

He waited, but when she didn't immediately answer, he jumped back in. "All right. You're not saying yes—much less 'yes, Cord, you're so right, I'm going to call my sisters this very minute.' So, at least promise me you'll think about it."

"I promise I'll think about it," she said, but the way she looked at him…he knew she didn't mean it.

Eventually, he forked over a pile of bills at the bar, found her jacket and raced with her to the car. The night had turned sweet black, a frisky breeze shivering the leaves; traffic had thinned out this late.

He glanced at her. "We're going…?"

"To my place. Not yours. And definitely not your brother's."

He nodded. "And as far as what you meant by that 'we'…?"

Sophie leaned back against the neck rest, studying his profile. She said with a bluntness she didn't remotely feel, "I don't know where this is going, Cord. I don't know what you want, what I want for sure, where either of us will end up after Jon's business is over with. But what I *do* know is that I don't do one-night stands. Ever. So you're coming to my place for the night. And that's that. Don't even try arguing with me."

He liked that answer, she could see from his start of a grin, the easing of his shoulders, the spark of fire in his eyes.

* * *

He liked it even more when she climbed the stairs, unlocked her door and then just wagged her fingers in an unspoken order for him to hand over his jacket.

He liked it the best when she threw both jackets on the couch, kicked the door closed and reached for him. Off went the sweater. Then his shirt. Her hands, on his naked chest, climbed up, over, around—everywhere. She kicked off her shoes at the same time her mouth latched on his and locked.

Caviar leaped on the couch top and plaintively meowed. She heard him.

She knew he counted on a heap of love and attention whenever she came home, but right now…her other tomcat needed it more.

She wasn't sure of anything with Cord…except that beneath the good looks, the brain, the alpha set of ethics, and yeah, the sexiness, was a sad man. A lonely man. He was around people all the time, but not people he could personally connect with.

That wasn't something she knew. It was something she sensed, from the symptoms he kept showing her, the symptoms that kept wooing her heart. His surprise at being jumped. His groan of vulnerability when she whispered in his ear, when she stepped back, took his hand and led him down the dark hall.

He might not know the way, but she did. Being her bedroom, naturally the carpet was littered with everything from books to cat toys to abandoned socks. But she knew precisely where the fluffy comforter was. She sank down first, pulling him with her, but she'd twisted half on top of him before he knew what hit him.

Cord clearly wasn't used to surprises—not surprises in life, not surprises from women. He wasn't used to being wanted...well, like crazy. He clearly wasn't expecting a woman who would yank and tug until she had him naked. A woman who would bite, then kiss with tenderness. A woman who could teach him to dance, nowhere near a dance floor. More than anything, he seemed completely unprepared for a woman who focused all her attention, all her heat, all her need, all of everything she had, just on him. Only on him.

Only for him.

He liked it.

He liked it all. But eventually, he seemed to feel there was a thin, very thin, line between pleasure and torture; at that point, he shifted her beneath him smoother than the slide of butter. The yellow bra, her favorite, was long gone. Her legs snugged tight around his waist, her skin a silken sheen as he plunged into her, hard and deep.

Until then, Sophie thought she'd had complete power over the situation. In a single second she discovered she was wrong. She'd always been afraid of needing someone too much, of counting on anyone or anything. She'd never thought she could let it go, allow a man to find her vulnerability. Prove it. Use it...for her. *With* her.

In another universe, a fire siren screamed and lights flashed and pale moonlight slivered through the windows on a cold, dark night. A cranky furnace came on, steamed dry air through the vents. She heard it all... but not really. There was only Cord in her world. At some point, a picture fell from the wall, startling them both into sudden laughter. They weren't just making the bed rock. Pillows tumbled to the floor, then her puffy white comforter, and then neither were laughing, because she needed too much. Wanted too much.

Yearned for far, far too much.

She hissed his name, then called it desperately, just as she started that long, long orgasmic soar. When the ride was over, she was gasping for air. He pulled her on top of him, where she poured like a mindless puddle.

He was breathing as hard as she was, damp with hot sweat, as she was. He yanked some kind of cover over her cooling body, but otherwise didn't move. Eventually, they both started breathing normally again, or close enough.

"It isn't real, you know," he murmured.

"I know."

"Nothing's this good. I'm going to wake up any minute and give myself credit for the best fantasy I ever had."

"Hey! It's not your fantasy. It's mine." She said, eyes still closed, muscles still like noodles, "Just so you know, normally I don't like this all that much. I mean, I'm okay with the cuddling part. I just don't like all the sweat and messiness."

She heard his choke of laughter. "All right. If you're going to bare your soul, I'll bare mine. Sex is important to me. Abstinence completely sucks. But seriously stupendous sex takes so damn much time that I wish I didn't have an overdose of testosterone. It'd make life easier. It's not as if I really like it."

It was her turn to choke with laughter.

They both felt a thump at the bottom of the bed. Cord looked at her, rather than the source of the thump. "I *know* we closed that door."

"He can open it."

"How? He's a damned cat!"

"He lifts up and turns the knob." She wouldn't have thought either one of them was capable of fast movement, but Cord suddenly swooped her into him, spoon fashion, so smoothly and completely that she never finished the thought.

"I'm not into sharing," he announced.

"Um...does that mean he can't sleep on the bed?"

"It means that nobody, but nobody, is sleeping between us."

That was totally okay with Sophie.

The dream was old, familiar, awful. A cold, dark night. Sophie, huddled between her two sisters, sitting on the curb, bare feet freezing. A fireman had draped a blanket over the three of them. The dread in her stomach was louder than a drum, so loud she couldn't hear anyone or anything else.

They were all crying, crying, crying. No one had told them their parents were dead. Sophie was crying loud enough so that she wouldn't be able to hear anyone tell her that, wouldn't listen, and no one could make her. But no one was even trying, until three strangers came up to them, two in police uniforms. One picked her up. She screamed. He carried her away from her sisters, even though she kicked and squirmed and hit. She had to have her sisters. Maybe she knew about her mom, her dad, but she had to have her sisters. She had to have *someone*. Everyone she loved couldn't abandon her, could they?

But then she realized, as loud as she thought she was screaming, she was making no sound. No one could hear.

Sophie woke in the darkness. She always woke at that same point in the dream. Always felt that first punch of unbearable loss…then exasperation.

After all these years, she was tired of the nightmare. All it ever did was bring the haunting sadness back. Throughout her life, she expected to be abandoned whenever she cared too deeply. It was old news, just like the nightmare was old news.

And of course, she knew why the dream had seeped into her consciousness tonight. She closed her eyes, snuggled closer to the long, warm body next to her. For once, she wasn't going to let her fears get in the way. Cord felt good. More than good. Even in sleep, his lips found her brow and his arm draped protectively around her.

It seemed that only seconds passed, yet the next time Sophie opened her eyes, dawn light filtered through the film of curtains. She loved it, watching the light sneak over the carpet, up on the bed, then over the strong orb of Cord's shoulder, his neck. She found herself smiling. Goofy or not, she felt as if she were purring on the inside.

One of his eyelids lifted, then the other. "You can't be perky this early in the morning."

"It's one of my faults," she admitted.

"What a shame. I thought our relationship could last a little longer, but now I'll have to give you up."

It didn't feel that way, judging from how enthusiastically Mr. Big Boy was pressing against her leg. Or, for that matter, from the sleepy glitter of arousal in his eyes.

"I don't kiss without brushing my teeth," she warned him.

"Oh. So now you give me the rules?"

"And I get the shower first."

"I should have known. The greedy, selfish side was bound to show up eventually. I've been waiting for it. What's the rest of the bad news?" He heaved a comical sigh.

She smiled...but then that soft, lush smile disappeared. She didn't want to think about old nightmares or current dangers, but with daylight, she couldn't avoid coping with either for long.

"Cord," she said quietly, "I know you've held back from telling me some things. You didn't mention Jon's autopsy results. You've never mentioned any details about your meetings with the police, or what you chose to tell them about what we found in Jon's apartment." When he started to answer, she put a soft finger on his lips.

"You know what?" she whispered. "It's okay. You could have all kinds of good reasons why you don't want me to know certain things—starting with the obvious. We've only known each other a short time."

He hesitated before responding. His eyes searched hers. She searched right back. Finally he said, "You woke up mighty serious."

"I did," she agreed. "And since you asked about the rules, cookie, I figured I'd give you the big-picture bad news." Her tone was still teasing, but she wasn't. Not about this. "I really only have one rule."

"Which is?"

"For you to be honest with me. That's the only thing I really need from you. Just be honest. See, I've always had a hard time believing in forevers. I'm not in a rush to count on anyone or anything, so I can sure understand if you feel that way, too. I don't need promises. I'll even survive if you choose to take off. But I really need you to be straight with me. And that's it. The only rule I've got. You don't have to tell me stuff you're not ready or willing to share. But don't mislead me. Don't lie to me. Okay?"

His cell phone chose that second to ring. She saw his look of irritation, but he scrambled to find the cell in his shirt pocket. Sophie could pick up most of the conversation from just hearing Cord's side.

His brother's car had been broken into. Like most around D.C., Jon had primarily used the metro—and his feet—for transportation. But Jon had a car, had one of those kill-your-mother-to-get-a-space rental parking garage spots with extensive security.

After Cord hung up, he yanked on his clothes. "I knew about the car, obviously. I hadn't forgotten it, but the rent charge was paid up for several months, so for a few weeks, I just left it alone. There seemed far more important things to look into than that."

"It seems increasingly obvious that whoever wants information still hasn't found it," Sophie said.

"Exactly." He bent down, kissed her on the brow—and without thinking, gave Caviar a stroke between his ears. "Soph—"

"Don't. I understand. The car thing is more important at this instant. We can talk later."

But when he left, moments later, Caviar climbed up on her lap, as if sensing she needed something warm and secure to hold. The cat snuggled under her neck and let out a thunderously reassuring purr. She snuggled right back, but it wasn't the cat on her mind as she scooped him up and aimed for the kitchen.

It was just Friday. A major workday ahead. She was finishing up the final interview with her Danish war survivor, after which she'd need to pour on the coals to do the intensive translating work.

But even as she started the day at a full gallop, her heart was on Cord. She really did understand why he hadn't readily shared certain things with her. A murder and murderer were at stake, for heaven's sake.

But Sophie was at risk, too, and she knew it. Not from a murderer. But from the man she knew damn well she'd fallen in love with.

# *Chapter 9*

Cord battled traffic to get to the garage, fielded a cell call from the faculty office—a student was ill, was going to miss an exam, needed a resolution—and then another call from the rest home. His dad had fallen, nothing serious, nothing broken—but could Cord stop by that day? So. It was going to one of those nonstop days when he couldn't catch a breath.

Back when he worked overseas in some mighty perilous, touchy situations, life had seemed far simpler.

Two policemen were still at the garage, fussing with Jon's car. Cord didn't recognize either of them. The car, typical of Jon, was an overpriced foreign model with a fancy paint job. It didn't look quite so pretty with the trunk jimmied open by a crowbar, its wires dangling like wet noodles from the security system. Leather seats had been slashed. The lock on the glove box was ripped open, all its debris spread over the seats and console.

Ferrell was hanging at a distance, looking as if he'd taken root against a cement pillar with his steaming cup of joe. Cord talked to the cops first, but they didn't reveal more than what he could already see. The garage had lights, cameras and a live security guard 24/7. Someone had still managed to get in, break down the car's security system and pretty much take the car apart, stem to stern. Even though Cord didn't care for the ostentatious car, he had to wince at the damage. After a good look—too good a look—he lumbered over to Ferrell.

"I didn't expect to see you here. I also didn't think the car was even of interest. I thought the police examined it after Jon's death."

"They did, and found nothing suspicious. But obviously the person who broke in was desperate enough to hope there might be." Ferrell stubbed out a cigarette and motioned Cord to move out of the wind, where he could light up another. "We need a little talk time."

"It sounds like you're buying my breakfast."

Ferrell shot him a long-suffering look, but Cord didn't care. He'd left Sophie specifically when he needed time with her, missed his first class, had his whole life disrupted—again—by problems that were none of his choosing.

The corner bistro where they settled didn't mollify his impatience, but the place did serve blueberry bagels and had damn good coffee.

Ferrell wanted to horse trade. After all this time, he finally gave up the name of his client. "Senator Bickmarr. Wife, Tiffany. They didn't have a marriage made in heaven, even before he got elected, but they put it back together for the sake of ambition, and they're both plenty ambitious. Whether you knew it or not, she was one of the honeys your brother videotaped. She wasn't having as good a time in Washington as she'd hoped. Senator's known for having a temper, also for thinking he's got a play at the White House in a few years."

Cord went for a second bagel. "So you think he killed my brother?"

"No. I thought she did. Bickmarr hired me to protect himself, his wife, their future. He seemed to believe his wife did this. The cops weren't onto her, because they didn't recognize her from the CDs, but there was her proven affair with your brother. There's her fear of exposure, and his blackmailing her. There was a lot of evidence suggesting she'd do anything to bury the evidence."

"But obviously, you don't think she's the killer, or you wouldn't be here."

"Correct. Where the police stand on the whole investigation, I can't speak to. I don't totally know. But I know where my people were. They're alibied. I'm certain. And because I had to be certain, I checked out the other initials and names and 'hint' words you gave us. The only one I can't get any clue about is 'Penny.'"

"I met a Penelope Martin," Cord mused.

"If it's her, that'd be peachy keen." Ferrell, for the third time, lit up a cigarette. "But I need to know. The more I look into this, the more I find that your brother was a grade-A bastard. The number of women he was playing, he should have had stock in Viagra. I don't care, you understand. What I care about is my people.

First job was making sure neither was guilty of a crime. Second job is making sure their names stay out of the limelight when the murderer's finally found."

Cord finally realized what Ferrell wanted from him. Ferrell had given up the senator's name in hope that Cord would keep silent about the senator and his wife down the road. Hell, his brother was the guiltiest party, so Cord wasn't about to throw ink stains on anyone else. "I have no reason to be a problem for your senator, or his wife. If they're not guilty of murder, anything I find related to them can go in a bonfire as far as I'm concerned."

"I figured you were a straight shooter. So I just need you to know what I'm looking for. What I'm trying to protect. What's at stake for other people—" Out of nowhere, Ferrell muttered a swear word.

Cord glanced up, to see George Bassett coming toward them. The detective pulled up a chair, plunked it down with an impatient look at Ferrell. "This meeting wasn't supposed to start without me. And there's a limit to how much involvement you're entitled to in police business, Ferrell."

Cord suspected that was true, by the law—but not necessarily true in the reality of Washington politics and power. Whatever, Bassett posted his elbows on the table and gave him the next earful.

"It's my stage now. You listen to *me*. Not him." Bassett wasted no more time on Ferrell. "This case is about to explode. If you didn't figure it out when you saw your brother's car, our perpetrator is running out of places to look. She's getting desperate."

*"She?"* Cord echoed. It wasn't a new conjecture that

the killer was a woman, but Bassett hadn't put it down in indelible ink before.

"Yeah. It's a woman. We told you, from the autopsy, that your brother was hit twice, once with a blunt object hard and sharp enough to push him down the stairs. Forensics came through with more than that. From the angle and strength of the blow, they're certain it was a right-handed woman. Above average in height, but not particularly strong. The height's not possible to determine completely, because there's no way to be certain where the two were standing on the stairs." Bassett revealed a few more details, but Cord interjected as soon as he had the chance.

"It's not Sophie."

Bassett hunched closer. "The only woman with prints in his apartment is Campbell. She was all over the place, in the kitchen, on his mailbox, in the bathroom."

"You told me that before. But she also naturally explained all that. She was around all the time to bring in the mail when he was gone."

"And that's part of the picture. All those home videos—almost none of them were set in your brother's place. He didn't piss in his backyard very often, looks like. But that's the thing, because again it leaves Ms. Campbell as the only one we can pin down as being inside his apartment on that specific day."

Cord quit drinking coffee, quit eating, went still as a statue. "He wasn't blackmailing her, wasn't sleeping with her. I think you're dead right that this is coming to a head, that the blackmail victims are likely getting just as desperate as the murderer. Which is all the more reason why you need to quit wasting time looking at Sophie. She's not on the radar."

Ferrell spoke up for the first time since Bassett arrived. "She could have been a partner in your brother's blackmailing...enterprise. The actor in those movies was your brother. He sure as hell was too busy to be holding the camera."

"Anyone can set up a camera. There didn't have to be a live person involved. You're totally barking up the wrong tree."

Bassett took a pull on his coffee, left a latte mustache on his upper lip. "She's got a handful of women friends she sees. Right and left, we ruled out a bunch of women we were looking at, all had tight alibis. But two names keep coming up with question marks. Penelope Martin's one."

"I know." Ferrell had already brought up that name.

"The clue was the 'Penny' on the list you gave us. Pretty obvious that could have been a nickname for Penelope. Couldn't identify her for sure from the video—she's brunette, of a size, of a body, *lots* of body, but her face is too hidden for us to identify her. Anyhoo. She's a lobbyist, into trouble every way you look—a suggestion of bribes, of favors. Some men would call her a ballbuster. Point being, she seems like a real weird friend for the mousy-looking Ms. Campbell to have."

"Mousy-looking?" Any other time, Cord would have laughed. He'd forgotten how he had the same impression the first time he met Sophie. She *did* have a gift for being invisible. It protected her, he realized, but now that same insight made him uneasy. Her skill at coming across as invisible could seem a suspicious issue, from the cop's point of view. "You said there was a second woman close to Sophie who you're looking at."

He glanced at Ferrell, who'd never mentioned that second woman. But Bassett had clearly come to horse trade, just as Ferrell had. "Yeah. There's this Jan Howell." A spray of bagel crumbs drifted down Bassett's tie. He flicked them off. At least most of them. "Something's off about her."

"What?"

"I don't know, but I'm telling you, something is. Everyone we've been checking out has a past full of indiscretions. Motive. Ambition. Secrets. Most to do with Washington. God, I hate this job and this city."

Cord blinked. "Then why are you here?"

"Because I love this job and this city," Bassett answered, as if this were obvious. "Back to this Jan Howell. She's not kosher, I'm telling you. You can't trust a trust-funder, always has money to blow, no way to track it. She's a party girl. Dabbles in art, in politics, in do-gooder crap."

"Well hell, why not just hang her right now? Talk about a suspicious character," Cord said, deadpan.

"Make fun all you want. She's not what she seems. And she hung at parties where Jon was. People saw them. They knew each other. And Sophic was the link between the two of them."

Cord said slowly, "Let me see if I've got this straight. You think this Jan Howell must be a murderer because her parents have money and she doesn't have a real job?"

"Okay, okay, you think I'm shooting blanks. But I'm telling you. You gotta get more information out of this Sophie Campbell. Before it's too late."

Cord heard the ominous note in Bassett's voice, stood up. Before leaving, he passed on the account numbers from the Cayman Islands. Bassett and Ferrell both pressed for the rest of the CDs, but Cord wasn't up for any more discussion. He had work issues he had to deal with; he needed to see his father; and damn it, he wanted to get back to Sophie as soon as he could.

The meeting stuck in his mind like porcupine quills all day, though. Bassett and Ferrell were still scrapping for information. They had plenty. They kept getting more. But the bottom line was that they still hadn't pinned down the killer. It seemed to Cord that one obvious reason was how everyone was worried about everyone else's business...only, no one was worried about Sophie.

Except him.

And by late that afternoon, he discovered exactly how scared he should have been for her.

Sophie exited the metro with a spring in her step. She couldn't remember the last time she'd gotten home this early in the afternoon. She wasn't totally done for the day. She really wanted to dig into some solid translating work, but she could still do it at home. And whenever Cord could pull free from his day's commitments, she'd be there.

They had a lot of conversations to finish.

A lot of serious, troubling problems framing their time together.

But they *did* seem to be together. A wonder to her. The hem around her heart was still stitched with worries, concerns, fears—reality. But she'd never felt like this before, for any man, and she was going to let her heart soar on Cord, with Cord, for as long as it could.

A healing, blinding sun brushed her shoulders as

she charged up the steps, unlocked the apartment door. Inside, she grabbed her mail, then vaulted upstairs. Talk about a silly mood. She all but danced inside, kicked off her shoes, started to hum—some silly, corny love song—and aimed for the kitchen.

God knew, she had to do a solid chunk of work. Yet she was still humming as she put on a full kettle to boil, set out a mug and tea, turned on her computer. "Caviar?

"Come on, Cav, I know I'm home early, but you could at least wake up from napping, you ungrateful hair bucket...." Waiting for the water to boil, she went in search of the scrawny reprobate. For a feline who'd prowled the streets for years, Caviar had certainly turned into a spoiled, stay-at-home slug—although he always, always came out to greet her, if only to whine and meow about her leaving him all day.

She glanced in the bathroom, where he sometimes hung out on top of the towels…then by the laundry, where he loved nestling in on top of dirty clothes....

"Cav?" Amazing that he wasn't snuggled on her bed—another of his favorite spots.

He wasn't there, either, but one glance at the rumpled bed made her think she had time to change sheets—the pink ones were the softest, but maybe too girly? So maybe the dark purple ones. And in the meantime, since she was already in the bedroom, she aimed for the closet, thinking she'd put on her lavender sweater, as well. She was pretty sure she'd folded it on the top shelf, where…

The blow hit the middle of her back from behind. The shock of it stunned her more than the pain. Knocked forward, she stumbled, her face pushed into the nest of clothes on hangers. Another blow followed the first—a blow that pushed her farther into the closet. That fast, the closet door slammed shut.

She heard the click of the lock—at the same time she heard a plaintive meow from the far depth of the closet. For a moment she couldn't breathe, couldn't think, couldn't imagine what was happening. All too fast, though, her brain started processing the crisis.

Someone had already been inside the apartment when she got home. That someone had hit her with a hard, thin object—like a fireplace poker?—and locked her in the closet.

That someone was still in the apartment.

*Okay, okay.* The thing to do was not panic. Figure this out. What to do, what to do…

She sank down. The closet floor was a mess of shoes and purses. Something sharp poked her thigh. A hanger. Her back still stung, the banging pain refusing to ease, making it hard to concentrate. A cold draft seeped from the cracks; clothes brushed her face and neck, and before she could find a way to settle, Caviar leaped for her, not purring, just seeking her warm body to protect him.

She stroked the cat, knowing now why Caviar had been hiding. Minutes passed. Then more minutes.

She heard nothing from the other side of the door, but whether her assailant had left or was still there, she couldn't know, couldn't guess. She was afraid to make a sound, afraid not to.

*It was a woman,* she thought. There was a second there, where she'd felt hands, thin hands, nails. Woman's nails. And there was a scent. Not perfume, but a familiar, woman scent, a shampoo or makeup product.

Not hers. But the scent was familiar. Someone she knew used it.

Instead of reassuring her, the knowledge that the assailant could be a friend, someone she knew, seemed even more terrorizing.

Somehow, some way, the person had to be connected to Jon—why else would she be in her place, now or before? And what the assailant wanted was just as obvious. Whatever Jon had been blackmailing her for. Or whatever linked her to Jon's murder.

It was like knowing the alphabet, yet somehow being unable to create a word. Sophie had clues but no answers. She had reasons but no means to stop herself from being prey.

Thinking slowed her heart rate, at least for a good two minutes. Maybe three. Her throat was so dry, she craved water. Her back hurt; she was cramped and chilled and miserably uncomfortable.

All that nonsense distracted her for a short stretch, too.

Slowly, though, it seeped in on her.

Panic.

Splashes from the past blurred in her mind, only the past wasn't a haunted nightmare this time. It was an echo of what really happened. The fire. Her parents trapped, with nowhere to go, no way to save themselves.

If there were a fire, Sophie wouldn't be able to escape. No one knew she was locked in here. No one even knew she was home this early.

She'd been to this exact same spot before—a place where panic was so big, so dark, so thick and oxygen-stealing, that there just was nothing else. *Cord,* she kept thinking desperately. *Find me. Find me, please.*

That was her last coherent thought before the fear sucked her in and took over completely.

Cord bounded up the stairs and thumped on Sophie's door. When there was no answer, he knuckled the door again.

After a third time, he turned around in a grump and dug out the key to his brother's place. They hadn't arranged a specific time to get together that night, so it was pretty stupid to feel his heart clunk. He was worried, that was all. Worried about the acceleration of events; worried about the cops weeding out so many suspects, yet not enough to pin down the guilty party—or parties; worried about Sophie's relationship with the two women on the cops' list, Penelope and Jan; worried that no one seemed to recognize Sophie for what she was—not a villain, but an angel. Not a suspect, but an innocent, vulnerable, incredibly wonderful woman.

The woman he'd fallen in love with—in spite of Jon, in spite of Zoe, in spite of every damn thing that was crazy and going wrong right now. Cord pushed open the door to Jon's apartment and stomped in. He dropped his jacket and aimed for the kitchen, to battle with his brother's fancy coffeepot again.

It wouldn't kill him to wait a while to see Soph. He just wanted her *there*. So he'd know she was okay. So he could tell her about seeing his father that afternoon. Almost unwillingly, he felt a smile coming back. His father was sore from the fall, but doing fine. Cord had dreaded telling him more of the bad news about Jon's past, but out of the blue, their father—at least for the day—had forgotten Jon. So Cord told him about Sophie instead. How she looked, how she walked, who she was, what she did.

His dad, even in the brain fog that tore at Cord's heart most days, had finally said that all this Sophie talk was getting silly. Did Cord even realize he was in love with the woman? When he was he going to bring her around? At the time…

Cord suddenly lifted his head, the coffeepot in one hand, a mug in the other. He thought he'd heard a strange sound. A muted thump.

But when he went completely still, the sound didn't repeat. He forgot it, carted his coffee into the computer room and started switching on all the electronics. The sooner he dove into every file and floorboard in Jon's place, the better. There was no talking about the future until this mess with his brother was resolved. Hopefully, when Sophie got here, she'd take on the books. He dreaded the accounting stuff.

He opened a desk drawer, scrounged for a scratch pad…then halted. He heard the same vague thump again. He stood up restlessly, listened again.

Nothing. Weirded out now, he unearthed his cell phone, punched in Sophie's cell. Naturally, he only got her voice mail. If the cops hadn't black-inked a worry about those two women friends of hers, Cord wouldn't think anything of it. She didn't have a time-clock sort of job. Stopping by the cleaners could have held her up. Anything could have slowed her down.

Still, he was edgy now, too antsy to concentrate. He hiked across the hall to rap on Sophie's door again. No response. Damn cat hadn't even shown his face. No light reflected under her door, either.

He'd barely crossed back into Jon's apartment before

hearing that faint thumping. It was real, not in his head. It was just so faint and sporadic. It made no…

But it *did* make sense, he suddenly realized, and charged across the living room. Sophie and Jon's apartments shared a common wall, the internal wall affecting both the living and computer rooms in Jon's place. He thumped on his side.

Waited.

And there it was. An answering thump.

Then nothing. No further response. Nothing from the other side, no matter how hard he pounded from either the living room or computer walls. Frantic now, he realized he had no key to Sophie's place, no way to get in. Calling the police was an obvious choice, but not fast enough. Something was wrong, he knew it. Something was really wrong.

He started toward her place again, then spun around, hustled into the kitchen to paw through his brother's tray of spare keys. He'd forgotten. Sophie had said Jon took care of her stuff when she was gone, so her apartment key could well be in the mess of others.

He scooped up the three that looked like door keys, chased across the hall, tried the first, failed. Tried the second, got in, called, *"Sophie?"*

When she didn't answer him this time, he put on steam, following the east inner wall of her place, checking the bathroom, then into the bedroom where they'd spent that extraordinarily unforgettable night… God, the memory of her wildly coming apart in his arms was sealed in his mind like a secret he'd never give up. Heart drumming hard now, he scanned the room, the wall…the closed closet door.

The mental click was instantaneous. Sophie, being

Sophie, would never have tidily closed her closet door. He tried the knob, readily discovered the lock had been pushed in, and turned it.

The damn cat flew from the darkness, pausing only long enough to brush against him. "Soph…" He didn't see her, wasn't sure if it was just the cat who'd been locked in the closet who'd made those thumping sounds, but a patchwork splash of color on the closet floor snagged his gaze.

He crouched down.

She was all curled up, motionless, her arms wrapped tighter around her knees than a taped-up package. Her face had no more color than a doll, and although her eyes were open, they were haunted dark, glazed with shock.

Her lips parted once, then twice. "I didn't think anyone would find me," she said hoarsely.

"I'd always find you," he said quickly, correcting her. "Come here, baby."

"I'm okay."

"Yeah?"

"Really. I'm okay."

She was *okay,* all right. Like someone who'd been hit by a bus was okay. Her eyes met his—her gaze hooked on his and wouldn't let go—but she was so frozen in that fetal position that she might as well have been painted there. In his head, Cord started swearing, every four-letter word he knew, strung together like magnets. But that was just in his head.

"We'll just go at this slow," he murmured.

Since she seemed to be having trouble moving, he did the obvious, crawled in there with her. He ducked through the clothes, through the shoes and bags and girl debris on the closet floor, and then just pulled her into him, onto him. Her skin was colder than ice. He sat there in the stupid closet, with her clothes dancing around his head and her shoes kicking him in the spine—but it wasn't as if he cared about that crap.

Her skin started warming up the minute he had her wrapped up on his lap. Her cheek crashed into his shoulder. She didn't unlock her arms, her knees, but she burrowed into him as if he were a nest. Her nest. Her one safe place in an unbearably dangerous world.

"I'll be fine," she said, into his shoulder. "I just need another couple seconds."

"Hey, we can stay here all night if you want. We can order in. I'll bet Chinese delivers to closets." He kissed the top of her head, her temple. Not come-on kisses. Not even kisses for her. He knew damn well they were kisses for him, selfish kisses, self-centered kisses—his need to be able to kiss her, his need to be the one who was there for her whenever the monsters showed up. Any monsters. Anytime, anywhere.

She snuggled so close, she seemed to be trying to glue herself to his chest, his lap, his arms. He stroked slowly, gently, down her hair, down her back. Gradually, her heartbeat slowed to a gallop, which was definitely progress—but worry nagged at him. It was starting to feel normal, sitting in the dark, cramped closet, with her clothes all over his face. Well, not normal. But it was okay. He could have stayed there for hours. Because it was her. Something about Sophie had rearranged his head, his heart, his life, starting from about three seconds after he met her.

Eventually, she found her voice. "I guess it's a little

late to keep it a secret. I don't do real well in trapped places."

"I think you're doing great. Any chance you got a look at who did this, Soph?" He kept his voice casual, easy. He didn't want her to know that he had murder on his mind, but right then, he knew he was capable of it.

"No. I didn't even guess anyone was in the apartment." Her voice was still shaky with shock. "I never heard anything. I came home earlier than usual by several hours. Maybe that was the thing. That the person knew my schedule, chose a time when I wasn't supposed to be home..."

The damn cat had parked in the closet doorway, was just sitting there, eyes glowing on Cord as if accusing him of something. The feline suddenly, furiously washed his leg, then went back to that vigilant sitting posture.

"The person...hit me in the back with something. I was thrown off-balance, knocked into the clothes. Then I was hit again. Then I heard the door lock. Then..."

He heard the streak of fear building in her voice, intervened. "Okay, that's enough. Let's get out of here. Call the cops—"

"No."

When he started to move, she clutched him even tighter, so he backed off. Even knowing it was nuts to just sit there, still, he held her, still, he warmed and soothed. "All right, Soph. There's no hurry. We don't have to call the police until you're ready to—"

"I don't *care* about the police! All this time, stuff keeps happening, and they haven't really done a darn thing! I want my sister!"

"Okay, okay, Soph—"

"I need to feel *safe*. I need to *be* safe."

He stroked, stroked some more. She wasn't hysterical. She was just…afraid.

What killed him was how he totally understood. A sister would help her feel safer than a cop—because from day one, the cops had done nothing to protect her. They were so damn dumb, they couldn't recognize the innocent from the guilty, for Pete's sake.

But that Sophie wanted a sister instead of him ripped at Cord's heart.

He'd failed her. All his life, he'd been a problem solver, a doer. Yet now, when something really mattered, when someone he loved was in harm's way, he'd failed to act. He'd been spinning plenty of wheels, but not fast enough, not effectively enough, to prevent Sophie from being hurt.

"Cord," Sophie said desperately.

"Yeah. We're getting you out of here. We're taking you to a place where you'll feel safe, where you'll be safe. Right now," he promised her.

# *Chapter 10*

Sophie woke up in the strangest dream. She was in a room she'd never seen before. A huge bay window looked over a giant maple in full fall color, its apricot leaves gilded by a blinding midday sun. The room had been decorated à la L.L. Bean. Plank floors were polished to a high gleam. The bed was big enough for Lincoln, with double-size pillows, dark sheets and comforter, and a mighty serious mattress.

The dresser looked like old oak, scarred and unique and interesting. Change was scattered across the dresser, along with a man's belt. Glass doors led outside to a semicircular deck. She could see a single Adirondack chair on it, a pair of binoculars on the deck edge.

She pushed up on her elbows, trying to fathom where on earth she was—but that small movement brought reality crashing down on her. Pain startled her. Her whole back felt tender and swollen with bruises. Last night came back in a rush of mental snapshots. Cord finding her. Cord furious with the police. Cord locking up and feeding Caviar and hustling her into his car. Cord seeing the welts on her back, swearing, swearing more, bringing her a pill and something to drink and…

The bedroom door abruptly opened. Adding shock on shock, there was her sister, striding in with a tray.

*"You,"* Cate said, "are going to eat. My God, I thought you'd never wake up. Don't worry about Pruitt. He's in the other room, pacing around, yelling at people on the phone. As if that's enough for all the trouble he's gotten you into. Don't you worry. I'll take care of him—"

"Wait, wait. How could you be there? When did you get here? What—"

"No questions for you. No stress. You eat. Then rest. And those are orders."

She'd seen Cate and Lily both last Christmas. Cate never changed. The sisters were all blond, but Cate wore her hair wash-and-wear chopped off, and she was typically dressed in worn-out, snug jeans and a skinny long-sleeve T. Cate looked sexy when she woke up, when she went to bed, when she had the flu, when she dressed up and when she didn't. She attracted men just by breathing. It was the way she moved, the way she was and who she was.

Cate was blustery strong, but right now she had circles under her eyes bigger than boats. She obviously hadn't slept all night.

Sophie kept trying to grasp how her sister could be here.

"Cord actually *called* you?"

"Don't waste your time making out like he's a hero. He's in big trouble with me. Big capital-H *huge*."

"He actually *called* you?"

"Called. Checked the airlines, paid for an immediate flight, had a car waiting for me at Logan, and a driver waiting to take me here. And yeah, that was nice. Not nice enough to justify putting my sister in danger. But I admit, it was reasonably decent of him."

"Good God, how many are we feeding?" Sophie asked, when she saw the contents on the tray.

"Just you. And don't even try arguing with me."

The tray was terrorizing. The omelet alone was big enough to feed a platoon, fluffy and pretty and stuffed with a half-dozen delicacies. Wedges of fresh fruit filled another plate. Muffins, pulled open and steaming, were dripping with melted honey.

"Now I know you're really here. Only you can cook like this," Sophie said, suddenly feeling a sting of tears.

"Of course I'm here." Cate pulled up a straight chair. "I'll give Pruitt credit for one more thing. He didn't even blink when I told him I was shopping for real food in the middle of the night—on his credit card.

"But back to the stuff that matters. Damn it, Sophie, you should have told me how scary things had gotten. All I knew about was the guy who died, not that the situation had boomeranged into danger for you. Now listen to me. I have a contract for a job in Baja. I've got a little leeway on time, but really have to get it in gear inside of two weeks. So you're going with me."

Sophie's jaw almost dropped, but that was a mistake. Cate motioned with a regal finger, indicating that anytime her mouth was open, food was supposed to go in. Eating was hardly a hardship, when Cate was the best chef in the universe.

"I need the money, Soph. And I have to admit, it'd be legally hard for me to break the contract, besides. But you know what? It'll be okay. You just come with me. You'll love it. It's a big old luxury yacht. I talked it over with Lily early this morning. She wants you, too, but that's silly. She's teaching all day, while you can be with me full-time."

"You both are wonderful. But I'm not going with either of you. I need to be here."

Cate studied her, then sighed. "All right, then. I'll give up the job."

"Of course you won't. That's dumb."

"You come first."

"You come first, too. But..." Sophie gulped. "I never dreamed Cord would actually bring you here. I mean, yesterday was awful. I was traumatized times ten, talking off the top of my head about how much I needed family. But I was just having a meltdown. I didn't *mean* it, Cate. I know you and Lily both have your jobs, your lives, and you can't just take off. This'll all get resolved. It *has* to get resolved. I just..."

Her voice trailed off when she suddenly saw Cord in the doorway.

She forgot the welts on her back. Forgot being trapped in the closet yesterday. Forgot just about everything... but him. He looked wrinkled and worn, as if he'd slept in his jeans, hadn't brushed his hair in hours.

He looked so good that her heart melted like Jell-O. He'd actually gotten her sister. He'd yelled at the cops for her. He'd been caretaking her as if...well, as if he adored her. As if she were the treasure and he was her personal pirate.

"Oh, no," Cate said, with an exasperated glance at the two of them. "No lovey-dovey crap while I'm here. *You*—" the royal finger waggled at Cord "—out in the living room. And you." The royal finger motioned back to her. "You eat. While your Mr. Pruitt and I are going to have a little chat together."

Cord had the amused sensation of being herded by a magpie. Sophie's sister couldn't tip the scales much past a hundred pounds soaking wet, but when it came to protecting family, she was a downright lioness.

"What in the hell have you gotten my little sister involved in?"

Cord walked past the living room, which looked as if a cyclone had blown through it, aimed for the kitchen. His Georgetown place hadn't seen this much chaos since he'd moved in two years before. And as far as answering Cate, there wasn't a lot of point. He'd covered the whole story when she arrived in the middle of the night.

She'd third-degreed him until well past 4:00 a.m., after which she went shopping for groceries and started cooking. Neither had had any sleep, but Cate was still pumping adrenaline. Cord took one look at the kitchen and just shook his head. He didn't know he even had this many dishes. She was close to a one-woman riot.

Cord wasn't sure whether to start with a broom or a shovel.

"You don't know about Sophie," she railed at him. "She used to be this effervescent little pain in the butt. Full of herself. Laughing, stealing all the attention, throwing tantrums if she didn't get her way. Just a god-awful baby sister. But after the fire, when we all lost each other…you just can't imagine. This old couple took her in. They loved her, but only on their terms. They only wanted a quiet little girl, someone who never caused trouble, never made noise. She changed. She changed to accommodate who she had to be, so she'd have a home, so she'd be loved. Are you hearing me?"

"I'm hearing you," Cord said. He had to give her credit. She barreled into the mess right next to him. She even took on the egg-crusted pan.

"I didn't know all that. But when Lily and I finally reconnected and tracked Sophie down again, she was a shell. All closed up. Well-behaved. Damn it. She's *still* well-behaved. Are you hearing me?"

The deaf could have heard her. She was cute, Cord thought. Not as striking as Sophie. Not as subtle. Not the woman who made his heart thud and pound and race. But he wouldn't mind if she were the aunt for his kids.

Not that he was thinking about marriage.

First he needed to keep Sophie alive long enough to ask her.

Staying alive himself might be handy, as well.

Cate took the sponge out of his hand, all but pushing him away from the sink. God knew, he was willing to help clean up. She'd been making a feast to tempt Soph. But apparently to Cate a kitchen was a kingdom. It wasn't about work. It was about power. *Who knew?*

"Now, let me tell you how this is going to be," Cate said. "I'll get around to leaving after a day or so. If. *If* you make sure my sister is in no more danger. I don't care how or why, I just want the murderer or thief or whoever's been behind all this stuff behind bars. And as long as you swear that you'll keep Sophie safe, I won't even ask what your intentions are—"

"My intentions are less than honorable, and have been from the minute I met her."

"Oh. Well. That helps some." Cate was clearly mollified for a moment. "In spite of all this mess, I have to admit, she does seem...happier. Even a little zesty. Impossible. Even moments of silliness."

"I take it these are good qualities?" Cord wasn't sure.

"*Damn* good. But if I have to come back here, I'm bringing Lily. And believe me, you don't want to mess with the pair of us. If you can't get the job done, just say it straight right now. I'll take her with me."

Cord had enjoyed the whole exchange, but he had to get serious before it went too far. "She stays with me."

Cate's chin tilted up. "That's not up to you."

"Yeah, it is," he said quietly. "She's not leaving my sight. I'm as unhappy about her being threatened as you are. But as much as you love her, you don't know about the people we're dealing with. She stays with me."

Cate took a step toward him, her eyes narrowed as if she were just warming up to a good, long, down-and-dirty argument—when both of them heard the bedroom door open. Sophie padded in barefoot, carrying the tray. Her eyes lit up when she spotted the two of them together.

"Oh, good," she said. "I was hoping you two would have a chance to get to know each other."

"Don't you worry," Cate said.

"Yeah, we're getting along like a house afire," Cord assured her.

Sophie thankfully believed them. Her sister being

there was better than a shot of joy juice, as far as Cord could tell. The two chattered nonstop, talking at the same time, arguing at the same time, sat on his deck draped in blankets, sat hip-to-hip for a three-hanky romance movie that night.

Cord talked to Bassett. To Ferrell. To a security company. Hunkered in front of a laptop with one of his brother's portable hard drives, then on the Net, searching for anything on the names they already had, trying to find more evidence, more information, anything new linking someone to his brother's death or Sophie's break-ins.

Through those quiet calls and work, he watched her with her sister nonstop. How she moved. When she winced. When she smiled. How she was doing, *really* doing. The caretakers—that'd be him and Cate—completely fell down on the job by nine that night, both crashing in the living room before some stupid chick flick was even halfway over. Cate, of course, hadn't slept the night before.

Cord almost forgot. He hadn't slept, either. And he only caught a couple hours that night, because he was up and at it after a few-hours crash.

He met Cate, bleary-eyed, at dawn the next morning. It was a meeting of the minds by the coffee machine. "She's insisting I go home," Cate told him.

"I think you've been exactly what the doctor ordered. She needed you."

"Of course she did. Sometimes a woman needs another woman—especially a sister. But I see her laughing and all. I see she's okay. *Not*—" there was Cate's royal finger wagging at him again, even though it was a wobbly waggle before she'd had her first dose of caffeine "—that I'm any less worried."

"I'm worried, too. Hell. I wish I were being targeted instead of her."

"I don't get it all. But someone sure as hell thinks she knows something important about your brother—that you don't know. That no one else apparently knows. This *has* to get solved, Cord."

"I know."

"I'm thinking—I'll get a flight out Saturday morning. I don't mind leaving. As long as I can trust you." Cate handed him his mug, took hers. "Which I do. Sort of. To a point."

Cord wanted to laugh. Cate trusted him to the exact point he trusted himself. Sophie needed no more dangerous events. Ever. For the rest of her life.

Particularly since she hadn't done a single thing wrong—except for being a damn fine woman with a little too much nonjudgmental kindness and compassion for others.

Like toward him, for instance.

They took Cate to the airport on Saturday morning, hit a store for food, headed back to his place. If he hadn't already trekked into town both days to make sure the damn cat was fed and watered, Sophie would undoubtedly have pushed to return to the brownstone... but Cord knew she was not ready for that yet. Plus, he needed to fill her in on a number of things.

First, though, while he carried the two grocery sacks from the car, she volunteered to make dinner—but beforehand she wanted to take a long shower, if he didn't mind.

He thought the idea was perfect. A shower would

refresh her; then they'd have a quiet dinner...and the atmosphere would make serious talk much easier.

For the first time in days, he found himself whistling. Stupid. Nothing was solved. Everything was still wrong. But as he scooped stuff out of the grocery bag, seeing peppermint ice cream and fresh basil and the whole assortment of foods he'd never have thought to buy... it just felt good. Being alone in a house with her. His house. Just her.

That rare high mood lasted all of three or four minutes.

She'd been in the bathroom long enough, so he figured he'd bring her a mug of something. Mulled cider. It was one of the things in the bag—a half gallon of cider, and then this container of what she called mulling herbs. He got it. It was a drink she liked, hot, on a chipper fall afternoon. So he heated it all, stuck a cinnamon stick in the mug, then carted it to the closed bathroom door.

He could hear the water running full-on. His intention was to open the door, leave the mug on the counter, leave before he let in any chilled air.

The first part worked out as planned. He barely cracked open the door before fragrant steam billowed out. He reached in and silently set the mug on the counter. Unfortunately, he glanced up. Even through the thick steam, even through the distorted glass of the shower doors, he could see her.

Instead of standing up, she seemed to be sitting on the shower floor with her knees drawn up.

Smells scented the air. Something like oranges and vanilla—definitely not scents he used for soaps or shampoo. He thought...well, maybe she was sitting because she was plain old tired. God knew, she'd been through enough in the last two weeks.

But the water was beating down on her head like rain. The steam kept getting thicker, harder to see, more pervasive. If he hadn't been spying, hadn't been right there at that moment, he'd never have heard the choked cry escape from her throat. She so obviously didn't want to cry.

Didn't want him to know she was crying, either.

She didn't hear him, didn't see him, when he pushed off his shoes, closed the door. If he'd had a brain, he'd have peeled off his clothes. But right then, he didn't have a brain. He felt like two hundred pounds of dumb male instinct.

Her head jerked up when the shower door opened.

"I'm okay," she said immediately. Sophie's favorite mantra.

He wasn't about to argue with her. He wasn't about to talk at all. He bent down, sat down, pulled her onto him.

"Cord…" Her voice was strangled, trying to laugh. "You're getting soaked."

He kissed her. Hard. Just the top of her head. Then wrapped her up so tight that it hurt his ribs. Damn shower blinded him. He didn't care. And she tried to say something else, something funny, but then out it came. Tears like a river. Fears like a storm.

"I just keep trying to understand. I never did anything to anyone. At least nothing I know of—"

"You never did anything. Stop thinking that, right now."

"But I keep trying to figure this out. Why anyone

would hate me. Why anyone would think I'd do something to hurt them, or was a risk to them—"

"No one hates you. No one could possibly hate you. And no one's going to hurt you again."

"But what did I *do?*"

"Nothing, baby." Hell. He'd have given anything to erase that exhausted, haunted look in her eyes. Roses. Rubies. Rivers. Anything she asked for. All that laughter and chatter with her sister had fooled him completely. He had no idea what it had cost her to bury what was really going on in her heart.

"I keep thinking about the day Jon was murdered." When she lifted tear-soaked eyes, he brushed the wet hair from her brow. "Something must have happened, Cord. I mean, something that specific day. There had to be a catalyst, some event, something that provoked the person to kill your brother. If we knew what that was, maybe we could figure out the rest. Look. How about if we find all those people on the CDs, those women, and just give them back the darn things? We could have kind of a mass mailing. From Blackmails 'R Us. Or Ex-Blackmailers Anonymous. Or—"

Okay. He couldn't take any more. She was trying to laugh at the same time her eyes were running with tears. She was scared when she should have been angry. Trying to make sense of something that made no sense. And all Cord could think was that she'd been through it before—her life turned upside down by circumstances she had absolutely no power or control over—so the whole mess was extra traumatic for Sophie.

Only this time, the cause wasn't a fire.

This time, the cause was linked to him, and he hated it.

Kissing her didn't exactly make him feel better. But it sure as hell diverted her. And if they were both going to sit there in the steaming shower, it struck Cord that this made more sense than he thought. Kissing her. Forever. With the warm water sluicing down, cleansing, soft. Her lips were slippery wet, jewels of water beading on her eyelashes, down her cheeks. Steam cloaked them in privacy.

She murmured something. A winsome cry, a song of longing.

His one arm had her nested against him, but the other traced the length of her, from collarbone to breast to abdomen to hip. He wanted to soothe, to reassure. He wanted to take, to own. He wanted to tease, to arouse.

Hell, he wanted everything. All she was, every way she was. Till kingdom come and then some.

"Cord..."

"Nothing's going to hurt you again. Nothing. Whatever it takes, whatever I have—"

"Cord..."

"Hell. Did I hurt you? The bruises on your back?"

"Cord. The water's turning cold. You didn't notice?"

Of course he noticed. Or he would have. Eventually. Maybe...

He flicked off the faucets, grabbed a towel, then two, to wrap around her. Peeling off his sodden clothes took an annoying minute beyond that, and the chill of air should have cooled his jets...but didn't.

He carried her into the bedroom, hooked around his waist, taking utmost care not to press against the sore spots on her back, but forgetting a small detail—which was to uncover her head. When he yanked off the towel, her hair was an incredibly silly tangle, but she had a siren's smile. A Sophie smile. The wrong kind of smile, if she'd been trying to quell his mood.

His landline rang in the other room.

Then his cell rang from some coat pocket somewhere. The way things had been, both calls were likely connected to murder and mayhem.

In other words, nothing important. At least nothing important compared to Sophie.

"Don't do it again, okay?" he murmured, as he lowered her onto the mattress, heaping the covers over them both so he could warm her.

"Do what?"

"You don't have to hide things from me, Sophie. Not fear. Not sadness. Everybody hides stuff from the world. It's how we protect ourselves. But you don't have to with me, okay? No more crying in showers."

"No more crying in showers," she agreed.

And then she took him under. He'd thought she was tired. And low. And anxious and depressed and more or less beside herself. But in trying to carefully ease her to the mattress in a way that didn't aggravate the welts on her back, he somehow miscalculated, because she ended up on top.

He briefly suspected she'd maneuvered it that way, but of course she hadn't. His Sophie was buttoned up, tucked up, and especially all closed up when she was traumatized—which she certainly had been. So it had to be accidental that she ended up straddling his hips, spread so far by his width that her posture was beyond provocative. It stole a man's breath altogether. And then she dipped down, damp hair spraying every which way, and nested kisses on his cheeks, his closed eyes, his whiskery neck, his mouth. Oh, yeah—his mouth.

She took his tongue faster than a thief, sipped and sucked, then did a wiggle thing with her hips and sank down lower.

She never learned *that* move in good-girl school.

She just didn't seem to get it. Who was supposed to be comforting whom in this deal? Who was trying to show that possibly falling in love, deeply in love, problematically in love, was happening here? Right now. This exact second. For her. With her.

Later he remembered scent, sound, taste. He remembered the luring softness in her eyes. He remembered her sucking in a breath when he filled her, slow, deep, owning that silken secret core of her…remembered her opening her eyes and giving him an unexpected smile before starting the ride.

It was a smile saying "I own you."

A smile suggesting she was about to discover things about his body that he'd never known himself.

She couldn't have forgotten the trauma or fear of the closet ordeal, or of anything else that had happened over the last few weeks. But it was as if the *now*, with him, mattered more. As if the two of them together mattered more. As if she turned the switch on the negative, and poured out all the love and heat and energy that was in her…times ten.

When it was over, he was wasted, stunned by the volatility of the orgasm—and even more by the connection to her. It took a while before he found the energy to open his eyes. When he did, he found her lying there with a sweet, soft smile on her lips.

Naturally, then, he had to lean up. Give her one

warning glance before pouncing. If she thought she could do that to him without retribution, well. They were just going to have to do it all again.

## *Chapter 11*

If anyone told Sophie a month before that she'd be eating, naked in bed, giggling like a kid at a carnival, she'd have suggested someone was suffering from delusions—and it wasn't her.

But it *was* her. A giant tray in the center of the bed was chock-full of delicacies that Cate had prepared before her flight home. When they'd finally awakened, they discovered that they'd completely forgotten lunch—and almost dinner. They were trying to make up for it now. First, there was a wedge of brie, with hot marmalade poured over it, to be eaten with crackers. Another plate had fresh, icy shrimp keeping company with a wicked red sauce. Then there was celery, stuffed with crab and cream cheese. On the side table, sitting together, was one wine and one long-necked beer. And one very naked man on the other side of the bed—making a gooey mess out of the crackers and brie mixture, but was it good!

"Tell me again why we're having this here, instead of at the table, like civilized people?" she demanded.

"We both agreed that we were never leaving this room."

*Until daybreak tomorrow, anyway.* Heaven knew, a heap of reality was waiting for them back in D.C.—the unanswered questions of his brother's murderer, the source of the break-ins, the repercussions of all the blackmail evidence in Jon's apartment. Sophie still had the welts on her back to remind her that fear and danger were only hours away, still waiting. But they both figured that getting back to Foggy Bottom by Sunday morning was time enough to gear up for the coming trials.

They still had a few hours. And Sophie needed these last crazy hours with Cord like she'd never needed anything in her life before.

"You know there'll be crumbs all over the sheets," she groaned.

"Nah. We'll just toss out this sheet and find another." He motioned to the containers on the tray that neither had uncovered yet. "How can your sister make all this fabulous stuff and not weigh five million pounds?"

"She loves to cook, but she never seems to remember to eat. You liked her, didn't you?"

"What's not to like? She'd kill for you. Far as I could tell, that's about the definition of a perfect sibling."

Her eyes softened. "She is. And so is my other sister, Lily. I just wish your brother had been the least bit like my sisters, so you'd know what that kind of love is like." She added quickly, "Cate said she'd left some kind of

French stew for the real dinner, but after these hors d'oeuvres, to be honest, I can't imagine eating another bite."

She looked at him, her handsome lover. Cord was so sleep-deprived at this point that she couldn't fathom how he could still be awake…much less how he'd… *performed* as exquisitely as he had. Twice. He loved her, she mused.

And no, he hadn't said it, but she didn't need the words. She'd known the instant he climbed in the shower with her in all his clothes. She'd known from how he'd made love, from how he looked at her, from how he'd opened his heart to her.

Still, she jumped when she heard the landline ring from the other room. She was relaxed, even happy, but even that innocuous sound of real life hit like a shot of adrenaline. It did the same for Cord. "I'm not answering it. There's nothing that can't wait for a few more hours. I guess we should solidify some plans, though."

Her blissful mood faded, but of course she didn't expect that euphoric high to last forever. And they did want to agree on a plan of attack for the days ahead. Although Cord had done several back-and-forths to feed and water Caviar, Sophie was still fretting about the cat being alone. So they agreed that they'd head in really early tomorrow morning—where she'd pack up some clothes, her work, pick up her mail, get rid of old milk and somehow maneuver Caviar into a cage.

The goal was for her to set up here for a while. Technically, she could do her translating work anywhere, so it was no hardship to hide out at Cord's. "And something has to break," he kept saying. "They've got more suspects and clues and information than Carter ever had liver pills. One of the leads has got to hit pay dirt."

She not only agreed, but being an enthusiastic coward, she was happy to hide out in Cord's cave. The deep bruises on her back were still swollen and achy. There wasn't a reason on the planet to put herself in harm's way. She wanted to help, but being victimized by someone who mistakenly thought she was a threat was crazy.

She heaped more of the soft, warm brie on a cracker. "Did you think about what we discussed before? That the day Jon was murdered, there had to be some kind of trigger for the killer, something unique that happened?"

"Yeah. And I think you're absolutely right." He took a pull on the beer, as comfortable naked as he was fully clothed. "Something *had* to have happened that day. Something that provoked the person into confronting Jon. God knows, any number of women could have been motivated to kill him. But if we could figure out the trigger on that one day..."

"The puzzle would come together," she finished.

"Sophie, we need to talk about a couple of the women you know. Jan Howell and Penelope Martin."

Cord's head was down; he was still opening tops, finding more stuff Cate had made for them. Something looked a little green; he put the lid back on. Likely it was petrified vegetables. Sophie, though, had gone absolutely dead-still. She couldn't say why alarm bells suddenly went off in her head. But something was...off. Cord's tone had changed in an odd way, become too casual, too careful. And he'd brought up the two names out of seemingly nowhere.

"Sure," she said. "What about them?"

Again, it seemed like an innocuous question. But they hadn't been talking about innocuous things. Sophie felt another whistle of unease. "Well, you know how it is around Foggy Bottom. There are a lot of people living there alone, temporarily—like for political jobs, or for the schools, or for projects with the government or whatever. There just seemed a regular group who grabbed breakfast on Sunday morning at the same bistro. You start to recognize people in the same neighborhood, you know? They made the first moves, I think. Made friends. I wouldn't say any of them are soul mates or likely to be lifelong friends, but they've been good neighbors. Good company."

"Like Penny. Like Jan."

"Yeah. And like Hillary." For someone who'd been eating like a wanton pig, she suddenly couldn't look at the food. And sitting there without clothes abruptly felt…wrong. She reached down, found his shirt on the floor, yanked it on. "They talked about your brother all the time, naturally. All the best gossip revolved around him. Everybody knew Jon. He wasn't awake most Sunday mornings, but he was known to grab a coffee there, too. What makes you ask about them?"

Cord wasn't looking at her. Of course he was still eating. "I just think that your holing up here for a while is a good idea."

"Actually, I was thinking that we'll be in Foggy Bottom early enough tomorrow that I could do my Sunday coffee klatch thing with them. They'll think it's weird if I don't show up. In fact, they'll worry. Besides which…Cord, they've been really good to me, like pitching in to help after that first break-in."

"Maybe they pitched in. But maybe that gave them an ideal excuse to nose around."

The comment startled her. "They're nosy for sure. Gossipy. But I can't imagine a reason to be suspicious of them."

Cord fell silent. She watched his expression, watched his body language, and thought he might as well have been stabbing her in the heart.

Before making love, before becoming so close, he might have reasons to keep serious things from her. Cord was private by nature. So was she. But at this point, he surely had to know she'd trusted him with her heart. With her life, when it came down to it. Yet every instinct megaphoned that apparently, that trust wasn't shared, because he was locking her out of something.

She tried a short joke, a laugh. "What? You think the police see Penelope or Jan as suspects in your brother's murder?"

His response was immediate. "I think the cops see everyone as a potential suspect right now."

She tried another short laugh, this one downright fake. "Next thing, you'll be telling me they think I'm a suspect."

There was just a flash of dark in his eyes. He immediately said, quietly, strongly, "There's no way you're a suspect, cookie."

But she knew from that flash in his eyes, from his sudden stiffness, from the way he jerked around for his drink—that she was. She actually was a suspect. And Cord knew of the police's suspicions.

She didn't say anything else, didn't ask anything else, couldn't, not then. Cord's exhaustion caught up with him, which was probably the reason he'd slipped with those comments to begin with. He crashed early. So did she.

Yet, on the morning drive back to D.C., Cord kept trying to make conversation. She answered him. She smiled.

Yet her heart sank lower with every mile. The glow from the time with Cord—his lovemaking, his caring, the shelter of feeling unquestionably loved—was dissipating like fog in the wind. She didn't doubt he wanted to protect her. She didn't doubt that he cared, or that their lovemaking had touched him.

But something was broken. And she was afraid it was her.

A watery sun peaked over the horizon as they reached Foggy Bottom. He dropped her off, rather than both of them wasting time finding a place to park. She said the obvious things, that she'd see him in a few hours after she got all her things together.

But the instant she entered her apartment and called for Caviar, she sank in a chair, feeling weak as dandelion fluff. The tomcat immediately prowled into the room, meowing furiously as he leaped on her lap, and butted his head under her chin.

"Okay, okay," she murmured. "I know you're mad I was gone. But Cord was here every day, giving you fresh food and water. You know I'd never abandon you, you doofus."

But the cat seemed beside himself, kneading and purring and nuzzling. Sophie closed her eyes, burying her face in the cat's soft fur, wishing the thick, sad lump in her throat would go away. She knew she had some unreasonable fears. She knew it was irrationally hard for her to believe that anyone could last in her life.

But Cord's behavior—his suddenly changing from a lover to a man keeping secrets from her—hurt like a raw wound. When the killer was found, he'd be gone. What had held them together was the danger, the connection to Jon. But he'd always had one foot out the door.

Trusting someone was always a choice, always a risk.

Apparently it was a risk he wasn't willing to take with her.

"Come on, Cav, we can't sit here and let ourselves wallow like this." She forced herself out of the chair. Whatever happened between her and Cord, her immediate plans were the same. She had all her records, and translating dictionaries and work to put together. Clothes and toiletries. For darn sure, the litter box needed cleaning out, and the milk in her fridge poured down the drain.

None of it should have taken more than a few minutes, if Caviar hadn't tried to trip her every step of the way. If he wasn't winding around her legs, he was dropping cat toys at her feet—or stealing anything that wasn't tied down, such as her toothbrush, which he actually took out of her carry-on satchel and started batting around.

"Cav, quit it," she finally said, impatiently. Naturally, when she was knee-deep in kitty litter—new and old—the cat chose that instant to drop a new toy in her path. "How am I ever going to get you in a cage to take to Cord's, when I have no… Hey, what on earth do you have there?"

She caught the glimpse of something small and black, rectangular in shape, knew in a blink it was a flash drive. "How did you get that, you little demon? Give it!"

Naturally, the cat took off with it, delighted when Sophie gave chase. She couldn't imagine how the cat had found the thing. All her computer supplies and records were safely in files. In life, she might be a wee bit on the untidy side, but she'd never been careless with her work.

Naturally, the cat chose to burrow under the bed, making it all the harder for Sophie to retrieve it. She had to lie flat and stretch her arm out full length—which the cat thought was even more play. Finally, though, her fingers closed on the cat's treasure. Having lost the game, the cat ambled off with dignity, to wash himself in the sunlight, as if he'd never cared at all…leaving Sophie to stare at the booty.

She used flash drives. Everyone did. She used several kinds. Everyone probably did that, too. But she definitely didn't recognize this brand. Confused, she carted the drive to her desk computer, booted up, popped it in.

Within seconds, she recognized that it wasn't her flash drive. It was Jon's.

The drive contained a half-dozen files—all women's first names—but Sophie only recognized one. Jan. And when she saw it, she hesitated, then clicked on the file.

The first image made her wince.

She didn't finish looking at all the images.

Couldn't.

For a while she couldn't seem to move, just sat there, trying to make sense of this new development. Jan had freely admitted sleeping with Jon, but until Cord's comments yesterday, Sophie had no idea Jan was a suspect. The file, of course, supplied a potential reason. Then she considered the break-ins, the times Jan had been in her apartment, whether those events could be put together in some way she'd never thought of before. And still she sat there—but not for long.

Less than ten minutes later, she knocked next door. Cord answered immediately, although his sleeves were rolled up, as if he'd been working hot and hard in Jon's flat. "You're already ready to drive back? I figured getting everything together would take you longer."

"It will," she agreed. "And I need to make a short trek out for some stuff. I was hoping you wouldn't mind if we didn't leave for another couple hours."

"No sweat at all. From mail to phone calls to computer records, I can hunker down here as long as you need. Just rap when you're ready to go." He leaned down as if to kiss her, saw her eyes, stopped.

Maybe there was a short, sharp glint of hurt in his eyes, but there was certainly no surprise. He said slowly, "On the drive back to my place, I think...we need to air out a whole bunch of things."

"Yeah, we do," she agreed, and turned around.

When she hiked outside, it was a leaf-shuffling morning, crisp and sunny. The bistro was only a short two blocks away. Right off, she could see a few hardy souls had chosen the cement tables outside, but the line inside for fresh blueberry bagels stretched almost to the door.

Most of the neighborhood group was already there. Hillary, dressed in hospital scrubs, had clearly taken the ownership of a table, judging from the heap of jackets and purses behind her. Sophie recognized at least a half-dozen faces in the line, including Jan and Penelope. They both spotted her as she was walking in.

"Sophie!" They shrieked hellos as if they hadn't seen her in weeks, and immediately demanded to hear the latest news about Jon's case. Jan wore a fabulous Australian shawl over a riding skirt and boots, looking artsy and elegant, as always. Penelope, for once, looked as if she were a tad hungover. At her worst, she was still gorgeous, but mascara smudges darkened her eyes and her hair was clipped up in an unbrushed knot.

Sophie wanted to slap herself. It was so like every other Sunday, the same whispers and laughter, the same talk about people, the same smells and tastes, the same scraping of chairs as they crowded around a table. No one looked different. No one behaved differently. If it weren't for the flash drive in her pocket, Sophie would never have thought anything was wrong—much less that her whole world had turned upside down.

Hillary was the first one to rise. "I was on call all last night, can hardly hold my head up. I have to go home and get some Z's. Sophie, you better have more news for us next time!"

"I'll try," Sophie said.

Penelope and two others reached for coats next. Jan reached for her jacket around the same time, but Sophie said, "Could I talk to you for a minute?"

"You know you can." Jan tossed some change on the table, stood up. "I'm headed uptown, rather than home."

"That's okay. I just need a minute." Once they were both outside, away from all listening ears, Sophie palmed the flash drive and pressed it in Jan's hand.

"What's this?"

But Jan's face bleached of color, in spite of the brisk chill. Sophie fell silent, studying her, at first trying to imagine Jan shoving her in that closet. Then trying to imagine her capable of killing Jon. Although Sophie knew it was hardly evidence in a court of law, the blanched, sick look on Jan's face told her the truth that mattered. Jan's conscience was eating her up from the inside out.

"As goofy as it sounds," Sophie said calmly, "the cat hid this. I have no idea for how long. Apparently, Caviar thought the flash drive was a toy. For the record, there were a few other files on the drive besides yours. I deleted the others. I don't know who they were, and didn't want to know."

Jan was clutching the drive in a white-knuckled fist. Her other hand was pressed to her stomach. She said nothing else for a moment, then blurted out, "He was blackmailing me, Sophie."

Sophie took a breath. "I figured that. Not because I saw or heard about anything else related to you. I didn't. But when I saw what was on that file..." She didn't want to remember what few images she'd seen. They weren't pornographic. They were simply...lovers' pictures. A woman at her most vulnerable.

"I'd have lost everything if he took it to the attorneys handling my trust fund. It wasn't just about the money, Soph. It was about the family name. It was about ripping away everything I had—"

"You don't have to say any more."

But Jan only looked more hollow, more sick. "I didn't love him, Sophie. But I cared. I never thought he'd... destroy me. And the more money he kept bleeding me for, the more frantic I got. I didn't want to hurt anyone. I just wanted whatever pictures or CDs he had. I was ashamed. Try to understand—"

Sophie made a dismissive motion. "Hey—I'm not your judge and jury, and not looking to be. I just think it's time all this got stopped. All the threats, all the harm, all the destruction. Before anything worse happens."

There was nothing else she wanted to say or hear—not from Jan. She spun around and aimed for home. She stepped in the street, heard the blare of horns, jumped back on the sidewalk. Yeah, her heart was pounding, but she kept thinking how ironic it was, that she'd been fine going into that meeting with Jan…but now that it was over, her hands were shaky and her stomach pitching acid.

Maybe that wasn't so weird, though. Facing Jan was never going to be as tricky, as hard, as unsettling…as the man she had to face now.

When she sped up the stairs, she found Jon's apartment door wide open. Cord showed up as if he'd just been waiting to hear her footsteps. "I thought you were just going out for a few minutes, like to a quick stop. When you were gone awhile, I started to worry."

"I'm fine." The classic lie, but this wasn't the kind of thing she could tell him until they could be quiet somewhere. She felt his gaze on her face, searching, studying, but she hurried on. "You ready to go? It'll just take a minute to put my things in the back of your car. I'm hoping you'll carry the litter box. And I'll do something brilliant to con Caviar into the traveling cage."

"If you have trouble, we'll do the Caviar thing together."

Doing that mundane running around helped calm her nerves, at least for a few minutes. Caviar wasn't that hard to trick into the cage, but started fiercely meowing the minute the door was latched—and he got really ticked when the car engine started. Apparently, he didn't care for car rides.

Sophie was just as miserable.

She'd intended to wait until they got back to Cord's—it wasn't that long a drive—but an accident created a traffic jam. They weren't stalled indefinitely, but Cord kept shooting her concerned looks. Every conversation pushed to engage her, to understand her silences. "I've got classes early tomorrow," he told her. "And the police left messages, last night and this morning both. I called the detective. They want another meeting tomorrow. I'll keep in touch with you by phone, so you know where I am and what's happening, but I may be not around until well after six—"

She interrupted him. She just couldn't wait any longer. "If you're going to see the police, there's something I have to tell you. Well. Actually, there's something I want to give you."

She fished in her patchwork bag, found the original flash drive and put it on the dash where he could see it.

"What's this?" Finally, there was a break in the stalled traffic and Cord could pick up speed.

It seemed like a million years since she'd made love with him, since her sister had come, since she'd sat on Cord's bed, bare naked, eating shrimp. She leaned her head back against the seat. "This morning, when I was gone for an hour or so…I went to Sunday breakfast with the group. Saw Jan, Hillary, Penelope. I stopped to talk to Jan afterward."

"You what?"

"There are a half-dozen files on that flash drive. I

didn't actually look at all of them, but I'd bet the barn they're pretty much all…lovers' pictures. Women. Posing for their lover. That sort of thing. Anyway, you're the only one who knows or has that original. I made a partial copy—a copy that only had Jan's files on it—and gave it to her."

"You *what?*"

Her voice got a little waver in it, but she explained in a steadfast and calm manner, about Caviar, about how she'd found the drive. "I just did a tiny, tiny change in the original I just gave you. Jan's file is a little darkened. As if whoever took the pictures didn't have enough lighting. All the pictures are still there. It just isn't obvious, in her file, who the woman is."

"Wait a minute. Hold it. Just *hold it.*" Cord almost caused a second accident when he jerked to the side of the road and skidded into a sharp brake. The tires spit gravel. Cars honked behind them. He slapped the car in gear. "I must be deaf, because somehow I thought you said that you went *alone.* Without telling me, even after all you've been through. To see two of the women we already believed were suspects—"

"Actually, I didn't believe that. Or even hear the theory until last night."

She watched, a little fascinated, when Cord rubbed a hand over his face. She'd never seen him angry before. For that matter, she'd never seen him confounded, either.

"So let me see if I've got this straight. You actually went to see the person who probably broke into your place—"

"Yes. I think Jan was definitely the one who broke into my place both times."

"And who could have murdered Jon—"

"No. She didn't do that."

"And you know this *how?*"

She'd never seen a man try to talk through gritted teeth before. As calmly as she tried to answer him, her palms were slicker than waterslides. "Because I saw her face when I was talking to her. That was partly the reason I needed to do this. So I could see her reactions. Although I was always pretty sure she wasn't Jon's killer, Cord, because…I kept remembering how that burglar had pushed me in the closet. How she didn't shoot me or stab me. She did what she had to do, so that I couldn't identify her and she could get away, but she didn't deliberately hurt me. And that's just not the way a killer would behave."

"Stop. I'm really struggling to grasp this. You tampered with evidence. You're aware that's against the law?"

She frowned. She hadn't really thought about it that way. "Not exactly."

"*Sophie!* The way you described what you did, it was *exactly* tampering!"

"Okay, okay. I was in a hurry, I didn't have a whole lot of time to think. Maybe I should have thought that part through a little more. But I just changed it a *tiny* bit, Cord. And this was the thing—Jan didn't really do anything that terrible, except want Jon as a lover, care about him. She comes from this old, landed family, where she could lose her inheritance if she caused any scandal to the family name. But this wasn't about her, Cord. I wasn't trying to protect her from what she chose to do. When I found that flash drive…I saw a chance. A chance to push out the truth. This whole mess could go on ruining people's lives indefinitely. If the police can't come up with any better suspects than me, I don't have a lot of faith—"

"So that's what this is about, isn't it?" he said quietly. "The police thinking you're a suspect."

She turned away, watched the gray-hemmed clouds drift from the west, darkening the sky. Cord slowly pulled back onto the road, started driving again. She wasn't going to cry. She just needed a moment to swallow the fat, thick lump in her throat. "No," she said finally. "This wasn't about the police thinking I was a suspect. It's about something more serious."

"Possibly only you would think something could be more serious. So let's have it. What really bothered you?"

She'd lied before. Who hadn't? When a woman was struggling to survive, she did whatever she had to do. But it was odd, how the darkening sky and traffic sounds all seemed to fade to a distance. She noticed a ragged cuticle on her thumb. Bit sharply at it. Even drew blood, although she didn't feel a thing.

"Eventually—hopefully sooner than later," she said carefully, "your brother's murderer is going to be found. But after that...I know perfectly well you and I won't see each other again."

For an instant, she thought he was going to slam on the brakes again, but beyond a sudden sway of the wheels, he kept on driving. "Why would you think that?"

"Because it's the truth."

"You don't think there's a chance that...real love, serious love, *gut* love could grow out of this mess?"

She kept her voice even and calm. "I think we came

together in a time of stress and confusion. At a time when neither of us really had anyone else to turn to. And it's been wonderful. I haven't let down my guard with anyone in eons."

"*But*. I hear the *but* in your voice."

*No, he didn't,* Sophie thought. She certainly wanted him to think she was calm enough to sound logical and honest. "*But,*" she echoed softly, "when it's over, it's over."

"It's *not* over."

"I realize that. But giving that drive to Jan was a start. Something'll happen from here. No one else will be breaking into my place—at least I hope not, because I'm certain she was the culprit. One by one, other suspects could be eliminated if they're pushed a little, too. Layers are getting peeled off the onion. The smell's out there."

Cord was silent for a mile, maybe two. She saw the turn for his drive. Even if she wasn't clear on the directions yet—generally, she could get lost in an elevator—she recognized the nest of white birches, the skinny creek gleaming pewter in the fading sunlight.

"Soph?"

She turned her head.

"I'm in love with you. Even if I want to wring your neck right now, I'm in love with you. We're going to fix this mess. And then we'll finish talking about this."

She thought that maybe he believed that. God knew, she felt love when she was with him. But when he'd kept so much from her, especially the police's suspicions, she felt as if something just...crushed...in her heart.

It was so hard for her to trust that she shouldn't have been surprised Cord couldn't find it in himself to trust her. She got it completely. It was life as Sophie always knew it. The only surprise was realizing that she'd still had a heart that could be broken.

# *Chapter 12*

When Sophie woke up, she was certain she had a fever of one hundred and ten. A few yawns later, she realized that she was at Cord's, that Cord was gone, that his couch was wonderfully comfortable, and that the source of the heat was the four blankets he'd heaped on top of her.

Sometime in the night he must have worried that she'd be cold.

Truthfully, the only time Sophie figured she'd ever be warm again—warm where it counted—would be in his bed. And that wasn't likely to happen.

Around 3:00 a.m., when she'd been staring at the dust motes on the ceiling, unable to sleep, the obvious occurred to her regarding Jan Howell. If Jan hadn't killed Cord's brother, then someone else must have.

She was relieved to have a place to hide out. It just

felt…off…to be taking advantage of Cord's protection when the two of them were barely speaking.

An oomph leaped on her stomach. The purr machine.

Caviar hadn't stopped purring since he'd been let loose in Cord's place. Maybe one tomcat appreciated another tomcat's lair. Caviar obviously didn't care where he was, as long as the food was good, he was free to prowl around, and on demand, he could get his share of love.

She loved him hugely…then made up the couch bed and started her day. Concentration might be tough, but she still had a living to earn, and God knew, piles of work to do. Her laptop set up readily enough in a corner of his living room.

She was translating Danish to English—always harder than translating English to Danish—when Cord's landline rang. He would have used her cell if he needed to contact her, so she ignored it. After several rings, though, the voice mail kicked in, and she heard a familiar voice.

"Pruitt. This is George Bassett. I know you returned our call, set a meeting time around one. Need to make it closer to three. And listen. I know you were pissed off about how we handled the Campbell woman last Thursday, but she's disappeared now, if you didn't know. Jan Howell, now, she didn't show up for her job today, either. Got more than that to discuss with you, but it's time you quit dicking around. Bring all the stuff you know on the Campbell woman. Let's get it all on the table."

That was it. The whole message. In the total silence after Bassett hung up, Sophie's heart was suddenly pounding, pounding. It had been such a slap, when Cord let it slip how she'd been on the suspect list for the police.

This was a whole new slap, though. The detective had clearly been implying that Cord was spying on her. Collecting information on her, that he was supposed to report to the cops.

Cord? Spying on her? The one man she'd allowed to let down her guard to, for the first time in eons? The one man where she'd let her inner, wild, impulsive, emotional self out of hiding, the Sophie she thought was long dead and buried? The one man who'd invoked the utter panic and joy of falling in love completely?

She tried to grasp it. That nothing she'd believed about their time together was true…that nothing she'd felt was real.

Caviar pawed at her leg, clearly bored with not being the center of the universe. Sophie bent down, picked him up. "You're going to get cat hair all over his house," she told the feline. "I don't suppose you have any more flash drives you've been hiding? Treasures? Money? I can't take much more of not knowing the truth, Cav. This has *got* to get over with."

The cat stood vigil while she showered, washed her hair, brewed a pot of coffee, and then hunkered back down in front of her computer in old jeans and a Smithsonian T-shirt and big old, warm socks. She tried working again. A couple of times, she gave up, curled up in a ball and just tried to wrap her mind around the whole situation, make some sense of it. It just made her more miserable. She went back to work.

When the landline rang a second time, she closed the door so she couldn't hear any more voice messages.

One step at a time. That's how she figured she was going to survive this day. But when a car pulled up in Cord's driveway in midafternoon, she was stuck with the interruption.

The striking woman who stepped out of the lipstick-red Mazda had an upswept hairstyle, kick-ass boots and a suede skirt to die for. Sophie saw her, took a breath and acted astonished as she pulled open the door.

"How on earth did you know I was here? Or did you come to see Cord?"

"I came to see you! I picked up so much gossip about Jon and Jan Howell since yesterday that I couldn't wait to share it. I just ducked out of the office and decided to play hooky." Penelope Martin rushed up the steps and gave her a big hug. "You've been through hell, haven't you?"

"Hell times three," Sophie agreed.

"I brought fancy coffee. And chocolate." Penelope lifted the gilt-wrapped bag.

"Good, come on in," Sophie said.

The interview room was enticingly decorated with dirty gray walls, gray floor and a gray conference table. It smelled of stale coffee and old doughnuts. Various signs claimed it was a smoke-free building, but a plastic ashtray took center stage on the table. In fact, it was the only decoration—beyond heaps of files and CDs and drives being run through the laptop that Bassett carted in.

Cord had been stuck here since…well, he wasn't sure how long, but it was surely in the ballpark of when hell froze over. Bassett, Ferrell, two other men in old suits and one quiet woman in uniform had been crammed in together for the same interminable length of time.

Bassett was so excited his jowls were bouncing. They'd been eliminating name after name. Bringing it all down, as he put it.

They'd tracked down his brother's illegitimate daughter. Now—or soon—Cord would be free to see his baby niece privately. Payments going to her, however, were established as child support. The mother of Jon's child was nowhere near D.C. when Jon was killed, so she was readily eliminated as a potential suspect.

"Lover" CDs had been viewed, dating as far back as seven years before. All but five women had been identified. The others had all been investigated, resulting in either the women and/or their spouses being alibied on the day of Jon's death.

"That's what the investigative end of the job is," Bassett said exuberantly. "Just plain hard work. Tracking down every person. The when, the where, the how, the why—"

"We've been here for hours," Ferrell pieced in. "You think you could orgasm over your job some other time?"

"I'm just saying."

"We know you're 'just saying.' But it's time to sum up. Everyone we originally believed to be prime suspects has been eliminated. Peter Bickmarr. Tiffany. The two senators we were looking at. The newscaster…"

"I just want to know where that guy got his Viagra," said one of the side detectives, who'd clearly come to admire Jon's prowess.

"Well, this is the crunch. We have no videos of Sophie Campbell. No videos, no letters, no e-mails, no pictures. But when push comes all the way down to shove, pretty much the most we have left are the names of three women who've shown they knew Jon, they had the opportunity, and who for different reasons could well have had the motivation to kill him. Jan Howell. Penelope Martin. And Sophie Campbell. Jan and Sophie haven't been locatable all day—"

"Hold it." Cord had heard Penelope's name before, but not as a bottom-line possibility. "You said there were five—"

"Two are mighty iffy. Those three are the best suspects we have. Of course, there are still CDs you haven't given us."

"Yet," Bassett said meaningfully.

"We're not totally through tracking the money. Unfortunately, your brother had a highly active career, Cord. You have to admit, he was a self-made man. One who carved out a lifestyle, a sizable annual income, from doing nothing but—"

"Hurting women?" He punched his number, the landline at home, said to the group, "It's Penelope Martin."

"What?"

"I'll explain—but I'm going home immediately. I always told you it wasn't Sophie. I'm equally certain it wasn't Jan, since yesterday—"

"You didn't tell us—"

"You've been talking the whole time. We all have. Name by name. I didn't realize it was down to the serious short list. But now, damn it, I do. I *have* to get home." His landline rang and rang. And rang. Of course, Sophie wouldn't automatically pick up his phone. When voice mail kicked in, he gave up, and started punching in her cell at the same time he barreled out the door.

She didn't answer her cell, either.

He told himself he was stupid to worry. She was likely just working, not wanting to be bothered with calls. God knew, her sister had left enough food for days, and Cord had no reason to believe Penelope knew where Sophie was.

He had no reason to be scared that she was in danger. But he was. It was so crazy—discovering that all the big money, the big players had not proven to be the guilty ones. Instead, it was the vulnerable women who'd been pushed to the wall by his brother—the ones who had no way to pay up. The ones whose hearts had been bruised a hell of a lot more than their bank accounts could ever be.

It was damn hard to speed on the freeways escaping D.C. He did it anyway. He kept thinking how he'd bruised Sophie's vulnerable heart. In that sense, he was no less guilty than his brother for hurting an innocent person.

She'd severed their relationship yesterday faster than a scissor could cut paper. Said logical things. Said them calmly, coldly, kindly.

She didn't mean any of it.

He just hadn't known what to say. What to do. How to make it right. He just had to maintain his priorities—which were, first, to keep Sophie safe, and second, to get the damn business of his brother finished. Then, he wanted to believe, he'd have a lifetime to woo Sophie the way he wanted to woo her. The way she needed to be wooed.

A black Mustang cut him off. Cord heeled the

accelerator. A local radio station had already been playing, the announcer reporting on wars, earthquakes, volcanoes and disasters. He turned it off.

He knew what disaster was—the risk of losing the woman he loved, the only woman he'd ever really loved. The only woman he knew damn well would be there for him through thick and thin.

If she could just be coaxed to trust him again.

He spun wheels turning the last corner at the birch trees, barreled down the road. He saw, with a punch to his heart, that a car was already parked in his driveway.

It was a girl car. Not because it was Mazda, but because it was a fancy red. Had a ton of bumper stickers, all political.

It had to belong to Penelope Martin.

He slammed on the brakes, parked right there, hurled out of the car and started running.

"Come on, Sophie, you haven't even touched your coffee—and I know how much you love Irish crème. Shoo," Penelope said, irritably, to Caviar, who seemed determined to climb on the couch between them. "Jan told me what you did."

"Told you?"

"She and I were friends for ages. We never kept secrets from each other. I gave her a key to my parents' place on Nantucket, so she could take off for a few days, lick her wounds. That was a kind thing you did, giving her that drive."

*Finally,* Sophie thought. She'd been waiting for trouble—the trouble that mattered—from the minute Penelope showed up. "I guess I'm relieved you know," she said.

"Jon was such a jerk. Jan always claimed she only slept with him to collect another notch on her belt. But the truth is, she never slept around as much as she put on. And the blackmail thing was a huge shock." Penelope nudged the bag of chocolates closer to her. "They're nougats. Thought you told me they were your favorite. Honey, you look exhausted."

"I am."

"You *must* have discovered more than Jan's pictures. Didn't you find a bunch of wild stuff? Did you give it all to the police, or find a way to give the evidence back to the women, the way you did Jan? Come on, you know you can trust me. How many did that son of a sea dog take for a ride, anyway?"

"Honestly, I don't know. There were just too many to—"

"I know what'll make you feel better." Penelope snapped her fingers, then dug in her lizard bag until she found a small vial of ibuprofen. She shook one in her hand, than handed Sophie the pill with her coffee. "Come on. I know you've got a headache. I can see the strain in your eyes. One ibuprofen isn't going to hurt you."

"You're right," Sophie said, and obediently accepted the pill. She'd avoided the coffee and chocolate. It wasn't as if she were stupid. Once Penelope arrived, it seemed obvious that her best shot at survival was appearing warm and welcoming—rather than scared out of her mind.

The way Pen kept pushing the coffee and nougats, Sophie figured they both must have been doctored. And because Penelope hadn't left her alone, even for two shakes, she'd had no way to call Cord or the police or anyone else.

Truthfully, she didn't expect the police to help her. Cord was a different story, but Cord wasn't due home until past six.

Sophie couldn't imagine stalling would work that long, so she figured she'd have to find a way to work with the pill. She popped it in her mouth, then faked a cough. Smiling, half laughing, she gestured to Penelope that she was choking, and ran into the kitchen with the coffee.

As soon as Penelope could no longer see her, she dropped the pill in the disposal, poured a little coffee down the drain and spun around....

Only to find Penelope standing there, tapping her five-hundred-dollar lambskin boots. "Hell," she said wearily, "I wasn't fooling you at all, was I? You were never as naive as we all thought you were, Sophie."

"I don't know why you're here."

"Oh, yeah, you do."

"Actually...I don't." Cripes, when all else failed, she might as well try some honesty. "Jan didn't say it directly, but I'm positive she was the one who broke into my place, looking for videos and files."

"She was," Penelope affirmed.

"And I never saw anything, CDs, pictures, letters, nothing—that had anything to do with you. You always said you never slept with him. There wouldn't seem to be anything he was blackmailing you for—"

"He wasn't." Penelope sighed. "You know what?"

"What?"

"I loved the creep. I had no idea he was blackmailing anyone. Sure I knew he was a player, but when we were together...I thought neither of us were playing. It was all back pocket. No one knew we were lovers. No one. I thought that was a good sign. I thought...I was different for him. That he was ready to grow up, quit messing around, settle into a real relationship. I thought we were such a natural pair. We knew so many of the same people, had the same values and politics and all."

Penelope dove in her lizard bag for a second time and emerged with a gun. It was actually a tiny thing, Sophie noted. Silver and black. Very shiny. There was just this little eye, aimed straight at her.

Since honesty had failed, Sophie was happy to try begging. "Come on. Why would you do this? I thought you were my friend."

"You were. I thought. But damn it, Sophie. You can't let anything go. You kept finding out more and more things. And sooner or later, I was afraid you'd find out about me. Jan knew."

"Jan knew you killed him?"

"No. Jan knew I loved him."

"Then why...?" It was hard to talk when a girl was hyperventilating. Sophie couldn't see many more options. Her back was to the sink. At the end of the kitchen counter, before the nook table, was the back door. She was in stocking feet, and it was cold out there, and she didn't know if the door was locked...but it was the closest exit there was. The only exit there was.

"You asked me why? It's all...because of the day that Jan came crying to me. She was beside herself, telling me about the blackmail, about how much trouble she was in. She only told me at all because she was desperate for money. She thought she could trust me for it."

"And I'll bet she could," Sophie said. "You were

good friends. And you weren't the kind of friend who'd judge her."

"Don't play me, Soph."

"I'm not playing you. I'm trying to understand. I never thought for a moment it was you."

"That makes two of us. I never thought for a minute that I could kill anyone. God knows, I never planned to. I came over, middle of the day, sure Jon would be able to explain it all. There had to have been some huge misunderstanding. I knew he slept with other women. But when I got there, he had all this…stuff around. CDs. Letters. It was his at-home afternoon." The gun wavered like a sick butterfly when Pen tried to laugh. "He was doing his blackmail accounting. When I got there, he just…smiled at me. Invited me in."

"And then…?" One more step. Sophie leaned back, as if she were shifting to a more comfortable position.

"I hadn't been to his place. He always slept at mine. He seemed to think that my being upset was silly. He put all that stuff away, locked it up, taking his time. I was just amazed. He had all these different hidey-holes and secret places, in the floorboards, inside drawers—he was like a boy in an electronics shop. And then…" Again the gun wavered. "Then he said come on, let's go to dinner. As if I shouldn't be upset. As if he thought I should have known…that I was just another lay for him. Special, he told me, because he wouldn't blackmail me. We were the real thing. 'Real thing.' That's what he called it. The real thing. So I hit him."

"I would have, too!"

"And then I hit him again. And again. And he fell down the stairs—"

Sophie bolted. She fumbled with the doorknob;

her hands were so slick, and she was petrified it was locked, but it wasn't. It wasn't. She yanked it open, heard Penelope scream at her. She started to run, but stumbled—she'd never been out his back door, didn't realize there were a set of steps.

But then she was past it—the three steps—then she was in the damp, spongy grass, running, hell bent for leather. A long slope of grass led to a fence in one direction, woods in the other. She didn't think, couldn't think. Just barreled toward those woods…

She heard a pop.

She ran harder. So hard, she was gasping, and her side had a sharp burn, and because she couldn't help it, her eyes were stinging tears. And still she ran.

She heard another pop. Heard Penelope scream at her again. Screaming, more pops, then suddenly… nothing.

Confused, panting, she turned her head—and immediately stumbled over her own feet and crashed on a knee—but not before she saw a shaggy head and a set of broad shoulders, tackling Penelope. A nearby siren screamed from the street—not soon enough, as far as Sophie was concerned. On the other hand, it wasn't as if she needed the police.

Cord was here.

Frustrating Cord no end, he hadn't gotten his hands on her yet. Couldn't. Damn, but what a hullabaloo. Penelope Martin had started uncontrollably crying, babbling a full confession even before the police arrived and cuffed her; then Sophie suddenly shrieked because the back door had been left open and Caviar could get loose. Bassett tried to talk to Sophie, to calm her, because the cops figured he had the best shot at getting her to spill the whole picture of how it had come down. None of the authorities seemed to realize that the parts of the story they cared about, and the parts Sophie cared about, were miles apart.

Practical issues made it even harder to get his hands on her. He'd seen her feet when she first came in...and pretty immediately, hit the bathroom to run the tub. It was no surprise her feet were bloody, with running over rough ground in the woods in stocking feet. She also had the mother of all slivers. She wasn't ready to have it taken out yet. She said she needed something tall and powerful before anyone—including him—came anywhere near that splinter.

He figured, when she asked for something "tall and powerful," that she was asking for a shot of whiskey. Instead, it seemed she wanted a glass of wine.

So she had her wine and was now soaking her feet, sitting on the tub rim. Unfortunately, George Bassett had chosen that moment to try to speak to her. Cord could have warned him. But didn't.

"You owe me an apology," she told George Bassett. "In fact, you owe me a million apologies."

"I know. We're sorry."

"*You* should be sorry. Not the royal *we*. *You*. Specifically, *you*. Thinking I was guilty of something, without even asking me! Asking Cord to spy on me! What's the *matter* with you? How could you be in that job without having any judgment about people? Obviously, Cord didn't know anything. He wasn't living here, had no possible way to know what his brother was doing—"

"We...I...know that, ma'am. Listen, I just need a

statement from you, and then I can leave you alone. We'll all leave—"

"I haven't heard my apology. And you almost let my cat out!"

"I'm sorry. And I'm sorry about the cat, too."

"You think that's enough? I've been scared out of my *mind*."

"I'm sorry. Very, very sorry."

She sniffed, but then seemed to relent. "Okay. I guess I'm sorry, too."

"For what?" Bassett's jaw dropped, as if disbelieving he'd opened his mouth. "Never mind. I don't care what you're sorry for. It doesn't matter."

"I don't think it does, either. Because I wasn't *really* tampering with anything important. I just—"

"Sophie." Cord figured he'd better interrupt before she spilled the story of her altering the pictures of Jan. He still didn't know how she'd done that, and wasn't sure he wanted to know. "If you'll just give Bassett three minutes, that's all he needs. Then he's gone. Then everybody'll clear out of here and be gone. If more comes up later, we can deal with it some other day."

Sophie was a lot more worried about the splinter. "What happens if soaking it doesn't loosen up this sliver?"

"Then we give you another glass of wine."

"Okay. Where's Caviar?"

"Snoozing on top of the refrigerator."

Still, it took forever. Bassett was a pencil pusher, wanted to fill in every detail right that minute, and spare people were still traipsing in and out from having to accumulate evidence. When the door was finally closed for the last time, Cord headed back for the bathroom with a sterilized needle behind his back.

"I'm too tired to do it now," Sophie said.

"Okay. Let's just have a look," he said.

She sighed. "I'm not good with stuff like this. I don't do needles. I don't do pain. And I've *had* it with stress of any kind. I'm not kidding, Cord."

"I understand. I know. I won't touch it. I'll just look, okay?"

"You won't touch?"

"Right. I'll just look." What *a baby.* Although he understood why she was freaked, when he finally got a close look at the sliver. The spear of wood stabbed into the tender side of her foot was almost an inch long. Three inches at least, according to her. It wasn't the splinter that was the real problem, he suspected.

He suspected the splinter was just the temporary, unwitting scapegoat for all her pent-up emotions that day.

He hooked her bare wet foot in his lap, an operation conducted with her sitting on the kitchen nook table, and him on the chair—with the cat now sitting on the table with her, to supervise. He saw the sliver. Saw it was going to come out just fine. If she just sat still.

She let out a howl worthy of a five-year-old child.

And that, of course, was when he could finally reach for her.

The instant he held out his arms, she vaulted into them. And that was it. She never said another word. She just held on and held on and held on.

Or maybe that was him—holding on so tight he could barely breathe, because that's how it seemed. He really doubted that he could breathe without her ever again.

All the details that made up Sophie Campbell, from the scent of her hair, to the texture of her skin, to the weight of her, to his terror of almost losing her—there was nothing else in his life but her. Not then. Not, he suspected, for the next hundred years.

"I love you," he said fiercely. "Love you, Sophie. Like I never loved anyone. Like I never dreamed I could feel love."

She reared back, framed his face in her hands. "You're honest to the core, Cord. I knew you weren't spying on me. That you didn't suspect me. I was just…scared."

"You had reason to be scared. We had a lot of people trying to play us off each other. A lot of people trying to protect themselves in ways that interfered with the two of us."

She whispered, "I lied."

"Yeah?"

"About walking away when it was all over. The mess with Jon is over, Cord. But you're not leaving me."

"I know." He took a kiss…then gave one.

She inhaled that first kiss, then took one back.

She closed her eyes on a long, soft sigh and settled into his arms. She'd had everything good in her life ripped from her. He was just beginning to understand how that built both her vulnerability and her strength. She'd fight with everything she had, past right or wrong, past danger or rules, to guard those she loved. Like him.

"Sophie?" Eyes closed, he rubbed his cheek against hers, sought her sweet mouth again. "I'll be there for you. Through bad times and good. I'll keep you safe."

She smiled against his lips. "Just love me, Cord. That's the only kind of safe that matters to me."

That, he thought, was easy.

# *Epilogue*

When Sophie climbed out of the car, she took one look at Cord's face and had to laugh. "Come on, you. How scary can this be?"

"Very scary," he muttered, and tugged at his shirt collar as if it were choking him.

"I'll be there to protect you."

"That's good," he said. "Very good. But I'm just saying, this may not go well. I'm not good in situations like this."

"Neither of us has ever been in a situation like this," she reminded him, and clamped an arm in his. They walked up to the door and knocked. While they were waiting for an answer, she rose up and gave him a swift kiss for courage.

The woman who answered the door was a tall, slim

brunette, wearing jeans and a sweatshirt. She looked at Cord first, and her eyes widened.

He didn't seem to notice her for more than a second. The cherub in her arms was wearing pale pink overalls and pink socks. The baby had barely enough curly dark hair to support the matching pink bow, but she was a solid chunk in her mother's arms. Still, the baby took one look at Cord—who should have been a complete stranger to her—and raised her arms.

"I'm afraid she's not shy," her mother said, laughing.

Cord took the baby, more or less because the cherub threw herself into his arms. He shot Sophie a look of frantic alarm, but she could see in two shakes that Cord and his niece were going to get along like a house afire.

Naturally, it would take a while to develop a relationship with the niece he'd never known he had. And the details of helping with support, now that Jon was no longer around to provide for the child, would all have to be worked out. But this initial meeting was just to… well, to reach out.

Cord had more blood family than he'd known before. And his brother may have been an unforgivable scoundrel without a conscience or a heart…but this baby was an angel.

They left somewhere around an hour later. Cord said nothing as they walked to the car, only crooked an arm around Sophie's shoulder and squeezed. It was only a week before Christmas now, and the neighborhoods were all lit up with lights and decorations. None, Sophie felt, sparkled as much as the ring on her left hand, but conceivably, she was a tiny bit prejudiced about that.

"Hey, Soph," Cord said as he started the car. "You want one of those?"

"One of what?" she asked.

"One of those little people. Babies. You know."

An early Christmas present for next year, she thought... Who could beat that?

* * * * *

*Harlequin Intrigue top author*
*Delores Fossen presents*
*a brand-new series of breathtaking*
*romantic suspense!*
TEXAS MATERNITY: HOSTAGES
*The first installment available May 2010:*
*THE BABY'S GUARDIAN*

Shaw cursed and hooked his arm around Sabrina.

Despite the urgency that the deadly gunfire created, he tried to be careful with her, and he took the brunt of the fall when he pulled her to the ground. His shoulder hit hard, but he held on tight to his gun so that it wouldn't be jarred from his hand.

Shaw didn't stop there. He crawled over Sabrina, sheltering her pregnant belly with his body, and he came up ready to return fire.

This was obviously a situation he'd wanted to avoid at all cost. He didn't want his baby in the middle of a fight with these armed fugitives, but when they fired that shot, they'd left him no choice. Now, the trick was to get Sabrina safely out of there.

"Get down," someone on the SWAT team yelled from the roof of the adjacent building.

Shaw did. He dropped lower, covering Sabrina as best he could.

There was another shot, but this one came from a rifleman on the SWAT team. Shaw didn't look up, but he heard the sound of glass being blown apart.

The shots continued, all coming from his men, which meant it might be time to try to get Sabrina to better cover. Shaw glanced at the front of the building.

So that Sabrina's pregnant belly wouldn't be smashed against the ground, Shaw eased off her and moved her to a sitting position so that her back was against the brick wall. They were close. Too close. And face-to-face.

He found himself staring right into those sea-green eyes.

*How will Shaw get Sabrina out?*
*Follow the daring rescue and the heartbreaking aftermath in THE BABY'S GUARDIAN*
*by Delores Fossen,*
*available May 2010 from Harlequin Intrigue.*